Also by Carol Baum

Murder on the Mountaintop Leads the Way

Murder at the Art Fair Raises the Stakes

Murder
at the
Museum
Paints a Picture

A Jessica Shepard
Mystery

Carol Baum

ARCHWAY
PUBLISHING

Archway Publishing books may be ordered through booksellers or by contacting:

Archway Publishing
1663 Liberty Drive
Bloomington, IN 47403
www.archwaypublishing.com
844-669-3957

ISBN: 978-1-4808-9779-3 (sc)
ISBN: 978-1-4808-9780-9 (hc)
ISBN: 978-1-4808-9778-6 (e)

Library of Congress Control Number: 2020920277

Print information available on the last page.

Archway Publishing rev. date: 11/30/2020

For Michael and Dan

1

A Bit of Blarney

The gray steel elevator doors opened with a soft thud, and Dr. Jessica Shepard stepped out into the dusky light of the hotel's top floor. As she turned halfway down the corridor into the entrance of the penthouse restaurant, she was immediately met by a single beam of light coming from an overhead gilded lantern in front of her. The rays hit her smack on and, for a moment, disoriented her. But that was usually the case whenever she was unsure of what lay before her. Taking some time to look around, she noticed that the illumination refracted off intricately carved, mahogany wood dividers, which partitioned the Asian eatery into intimate dining spaces, and she knew, without a doubt, that they would offer the seclusion Tom Martine had obviously felt necessary for the luncheon.

As she accustomed herself to the conflicting tones of dark and light, a hostess approached her out of the recesses of the restaurant. The woman wore a formfitting scarlet-red dress. Jessica wondered if the provocative attire was another reason Tom had selected this particular environment for their meeting. He liked to enjoy himself—whatever the circumstances. The satiny fabric the hostess wore was punctuated in strategically scattered points by gold-threaded embroidery, most noticeable around the daringly low, scooped neckline.

Jessica instinctively looked down at her own ensemble to compare it; the contrast was striking. Unlike the hostess, Jessica was clad in muted colors, as was her custom. The light gray slacks complemented her trim figure, as did the ivory silk blouse—its cross-body form kept in place by a pale blue cashmere sweater that cascaded down softly from her shoulders.

Although her garments did not provide the aura of exotic mystery of the hostess's garb, vibrant color was not lacking, as it was provided by the healthy shine of Jessica's dark brown shoulder-length hair that fell about her neck. Happily for Jessica, any insecure thoughts, which might have been at odds with her habit of valuing mind over body, were shattered by noticing that all the hostesses she saw in the restaurant were clad in the very same outfit; she was consoled that her own appearance, however less dramatic, was at least her own.

"Good afternoon," the hostess said in a surprisingly brisk and efficient diction. The sound of the woman's voice shattered any illusion of mystery; it was an accent clearly belonging in any of the five boroughs of New York City.

"Hello, I'm Jessica Shepard. I'm lunching with Tom Martine today. Has he arrived yet?"

"Welcome. Mr. Martine has already arrived and is seated in the back. He asked me specifically to keep an eye out for you and bring you to him as soon as you got here. He's quite a regular, so we have his routine down pat. We keep the recessed booth in the back on the ready whenever he wants it."

"Well, I guess that's convenient. If you lead, I will follow." Jessica walked behind the hostess, twisting and turning around the various eating spaces, as the sheen of the woman's scarlet dress provided a guiding beacon to follow. The few other patrons eating at this time of day—too late for lunch and too early for dinner—took no notice of them as they passed by. Jessica wondered what Tom could possibly want to discuss with her that would merit such intimacy. He had refused to give her any hints when he had contacted her by phone.

She had known Tom Martine for the past few years. She met him at a Saturday evening cocktail party for a charitable event that a Connecticut neighbor had championed. It was held in her neighbor's pied-à-terre, a private penthouse residence in New York City, not far from where she was now meeting Tom. At that time, she had been admiring the Manhattan skyline, illuminated at night, and marveling at how such a grand city apartment could possibly be anyone's pied-à-terre. Tom had approached her and graciously offered her a flute of champagne.

Tom was a freelance investigative journalist, and he had been so for enough good years to make him a presence in his own profession. He was known for his honesty and for his ability to get the bare facts. He was not one to shy away from politically incorrect truths and seemed to take pride in ruffling feathers—the particular pigeon didn't matter; in fact, the fatter the bird, the more likely he was to go after it.

But that night he had seemed out of place, as she had. And he had obviously sought out another duck in a pond of swans. Her first impression of him was that he would have looked more comfortable holding a pint of beer rather than a flute of champagne in his large fingers; those digits were more likely to be used to clack out syntax on computer keys. She also noticed his fingertips were darkened by cigarette stains. That had bothered her medical instincts, but she had held her tongue.

"You also look out of place here," he said.

"More than you know," she replied.

"So what are you doing here? Somehow you don't look as

though this is where you want to be spending your Saturday night."

"Being a good neighbor. Our hostess also has a house in Connecticut, close to mine. She thought I might like to attend her event. It's for a good cause. I didn't want to disappoint her by not showing up. So here I am. What about you?"

"Ah, yes, being a good neighbor. That's always important. Me too, in a way. But a Manhattan one. Actually, though, I like to attend these—not only for the moral kudos I earn by just being here, mind you, but also for what I may learn at the same time. You see, I write articles about corporate corruption, and occasionally I have to wine and dine with the best of them." He laughed before suddenly turning serious. Then he'd said somberly, "That way I can learn what I need to know when their guards are down. You know what I mean? With drinks in hand, the tongue often loosens. Luckily, my good old liver allows me to have the luxury of listening more than talking. But don't worry; your secrets are safe with me. I can be very discreet."

"That's an unusual quality in a journalist."

"Oh, don't get me wrong. I can be discreet when I *want* to and"—he paused slightly—"indiscreet when I *need* to."

"You mean the other way around, don't you?"

"Do I?"

Jessica decided it was maybe a little too early in the evening to indulge his repartee. So she merely said, "I think I do understand you. I must admit—you look like you'd rather be at a bar or a pub right now."

"Now you sound like my silver-haired Irish grandmother, darling. Or she would say *macushla*."

Jessica would later learn that Tom also had an Irish mother, an Italian father, and an extended family of which he was most proud. He had felt it his duty to not only chase stories but make himself personally responsible for the well-being of each and every member of his extended clan. He was especially close to his younger sister, Lucy, who was nearest to his age.

Now here she was meeting him, after all this time, and Tom had only mentioned in his phone call that their meeting was regarding his sister, Lucy. He had not provided any further details and had left Jessica to fret over what it could be about. Something in the tone of his voice, even transmitted over the phone line, had suggested that the matter was not to be a pleasant one. And now, as the hostess led her on through the depths of the restaurant, she was even more certain of it.

Jessica was an immunologist by training. She hoped that it wasn't that Lucy had been afflicted with a serious medical illness and that Tom was probing for some advice. But she couldn't imagine why, with all Tom's contacts, he would have reached out to her. As she finally saw his table, she discerned in the furrowing of his brow that something significant was definitely bothering him.

At first, Tom didn't notice her approach, so Jessica had a few moments to observe him unguardedly. He still wore his overlong hair brushed back from his forehead; the dark brown locks with just a hint of gray in them ran over the nape of his neck as though he had no time for such a mundane necessity as visiting a barbershop. She was relieved that it didn't appear he had lost much weight; he still seemed to have the same rugged physique she remembered from last seeing him. He was wearing a brown suit, which looked like it had served him well for some time, and the jacket had deep creases at the elbows: another marker of his writer's arms. She was shocked to see a tie around his neck, which was poking out of his unbuttoned collar.

"Hello, Tom. It's good to see you. It's been a while. I'm

glad we could get together this way. I've never been to this restaurant."

"Hello, Jessica. I come here often. They know my routine."

"So I've heard." Jessica looked around at the secluded table, enshrouded by those dark mahogany partitions she had noticed when she first came into the restaurant. Even at that time of day, a small candle was installed in the middle of the table and served to add some needed illumination. It shone a small spotlight on Tom's face, and he smiled at her. She tried to read his expression but couldn't. She'd just wait to see what he had to say and what he wanted from her.

"Thanks for coming," he began. "I appreciate your making the time to see me."

"Not at all. I had nothing pressing, and I enjoy coming into the city from time to time, especially to see an old friend."

"I hope you'll still feel that way later."

Jessica looked at him for a clue as to what he meant, but he only got up and pulled out the chair across from him for her to sit down. As if in choreographic motion, the hostess silently backed away in a manner Jessica assumed had been practiced many times before.

"So why the mystery, Tom? What's this all about? It's time to let me in on the secret, whatever it is."

"Well I'll tell you in good time, darling, but first let's decide what to order. I'm hungry, and the food here is excellent."

Jessica stifled her irritation and let him have his way. He hid his face behind the large leather menu to methodically survey the items printed on the pages that he turned over. Jessica was not fooled by the maneuver she perceived was meant to maintain his control; Jessica knew him well enough, even after some time, to discern that this attempt at normalcy was his way of organizing his thoughts. Yes, she would give him some time and see what it was he wanted to discuss with her.

After what seemed to her to be an inordinate number of minutes to decide what they would eat, considering this was a frequent haunt of Tom's, he finally spoke. "You remember my sister, Lucy, don't you? I know I've spoken about her, although you haven't met her."

"Of course, I do. You've often spoken to me about her. How is she doing?" And after an uncomfortable moment, she added, "Isn't she well?"

"Well, actually no. She isn't."

"Oh, Tom, I'm so sorry. I didn't know. What's wrong? Is there any way I can help? You know I'll do anything I can to help."

"Thank you. Yes, as a matter of fact there is something you can do. But let me get to it in my way." Again, he waited, collecting his thoughts before continuing. "Lucy and I, being closest in age, were always together. I think you knew that. But what you didn't know was that a while ago my mother was treated for breast cancer. My mother didn't want anyone to know, so don't be mad at me that I didn't confide in you at the time. She's of the old school in that way. But she did agree to the latest treatment, and as part of it she had a genetic test to assess her risk for developing another breast or ovarian cancer: the genetic test was positive. Long story short, my sister also had the test, and hers was also positive, and she chose preventive gynecologic surgery. So now Lucy can't have any children."

"Tom, I'm really sorry. It must be very hard for her. Particularly, with you having such a large, close family."

"Well, you haven't heard the whole story. The kicker is that recently we learned that the particular lab she used didn't have a large enough database to be as accurate as it ought to be; so maybe she wasn't at as high a risk as she thought, and maybe she made a mistake by precipitously rushing to act."

"What did the genetics counselor say about it?" Jessica asked softly.

"That, if it was any consolation to her, as the database grew, she might find out she made the right decision after all."

"Tom, that may be true. Genetics isn't so clear cut. There are shades of gray."

"But that's just it. When I heard about this, I made her get tested with a couple of other labs, and both of their results were different from what the original lab had found. So I started looking into that original lab. I poked around and spoke to some folks who left employment there because they didn't feel comfortable with some of the goings-on there. Then I started looking into who were some of the investors behind the company."

"Did you find anything that concerned you?" Jessica asked, still not exactly sure how Tom thought she would be able to help him.

"Yes, I did. And talk about coincidences! Remember when you mentioned a 'friend' who was visiting his daughter in Paris this summer while the girl interned at a museum?" For the first time since he had begun to speak, Tom's face relaxed into a knowing smile, which Jessica knew only too well from memory.

"Alain Raynaud?" Jessica asked, ignoring Tom's sarcastic use of the word *friend*.

"The very one I'm talking about."

"You're not suggesting that Alain is an investor in this lab, are you?" Skepticism was clear in Jessica's tone of voice.

"No. No. Not at all. Don't worry about that. That's not what I'm saying. No. The name I dug up is Frédéric Averi."

"Who's he? I've never heard of him—at least that I can remember."

"I didn't expect you to. He's a French industrialist. He has his fingers in many pots. He owns or invests in all types of companies around the globe. And, by the way, if that wasn't enough, I've learned he's also now consumed with a large château in the French countryside that he arranges tours to, rents out for weddings and events—those kinds of things. He also has a private art museum in Paris. The museum is but the latest in a string of Paris cultural venues financed by and revolving around a financier's private collection. It's apparently now quite 'the thing.' This one's called—"

"Ah. Now I see," Jessica said, cutting him off. "And not to be too dense, I gather Musée Averi, where Alain's daughter, Odette, just happens to be interning this summer, is one and the same museum that Averi owns."

"You've got it, darling. You're not dense. By no means, or I wouldn't be having lunch with you."

Jessica reached into her purse and pulled out her cell phone. Running through her recent text messages, she easily located one she had received from Alain, which she had briefly mentioned to Tom when they had spoken. With it was attached a photo of Musée Averi. She held up the photo after expanding it and practically shoved it under Tom's broad nose before taking her phone back. Then she looked more closely at the museum that Alain had described in his text to her. He had written that his teenage daughter had secured a coveted internship to work there for the summer. He had also suggested that Jessica might like to spend some time in Paris while he was caretaker of his daughter; his ex-wife and her new husband would be on vacation away from Paris. Alain was hoping Jessica would consider it. She transferred the phone back to her purse.

"Tom, even if I did agree—and, mind you, I haven't said that I would go to Paris to see what I could find out about

Averi—I couldn't involve Odette Raynaud in this. It wouldn't be right. She's only a teenager."

"But I'm not asking you to do that necessarily. All I'm suggesting is that sometimes when a thing miraculously falls into your lap, like this has, you have to take advantage of the situation."

"I can see you getting ready to make this all sound like the simplest of things."

"Well, it is, darling. Look. This is how I see it: I've got a very depressed, younger sister who I've got to help to get out of a deep slump. And I'm sure you do too, knowing you as I do. If Averi is on the up-and-up, fine. No problem. Then at least I can relax on that point. But, if he's just a profit hound and people are getting hurt because of it, wouldn't you want to do something about it? I know you would. If you go to Paris— which I'm sure you would have ended up doing anyway—and meet up with Raynaud and his daughter, you'll probably find an easy way of insinuating yourself into Averi's museum without necessarily getting Odette involved, at least without her agreement. And you'll be able to kill two birds with one stone, as they say. And from there, we can see where it takes you."

Jessica waited a minute, digesting what Tom had proposed, and then said resolutely, "I would have to let Alain know something about this."

"That goes without saying. From what I've learned about him from you, I trust him already. I really do. All right?"

"All right. Now, let's order. Now I'm hungry. At least you can feed me after I've agreed to be your eyes and ears."

"And they are very attractive eyes and ears, darling," Tom finished with all the charm and blarney he had learned to exude while cajoling his prior and current victims into doing whatever he wanted.

2

A Paris Welcome

The plane readied itself for landing at Paris Charles de Gaulle Airport, northeast of the city. It had been a long and tedious flight with Jessica sandwiched between two couples, each of which had decided to pass the duration of the flight by watching movies projected on the backs of the seats in front of them. Jessica had gratefully accepted the brilliantly decorated eye patches given to her by an airline attendant, which she used to cover her eyes and eventually drifted off to a deep sleep. When she was finally awakened by the sound of the beeping lights over her head, she did so with a start. After removing the eye patches, she was relieved to see that the lights were only on to indicate that the plane was finally beginning to make its descent into Paris.

Putting her seat back into the upright position, she eagerly awaited the plane touching ground and the opportunity to at last escape from her close quarters. Once finally off the plane, though, how could she fail but to feel a rush of excitement course through her with the knowledge that she was now actually in the city of lights. Everything around her seemed to scream out *Paris*, from the advertisements lining the walls of the terminal to the distinctive French inflections of the many voices surrounding her as she moved with them like a salmon up a stream. All of the fatigue that had enveloped her in the plane dissipated as rapidly as a vanishing mist, swept away by her newfound enthusiasm, and she hurried forward, dragging her rolling suitcase behind her. After Jessica cleared French customs, she began to scan the faces of the multitudes of people who were packed tightly into the airport arrivals area and who were also looking for familial faces entering Paris.

"Harry, did you remember to check with the hotel to make sure they would have someone here to pick us up?"

Jessica looked to her right to see one of the couples who had been sitting next to her on the flight. Now that she was no longer squeezed in next to them, she could feel a sense of camaraderie with other Americans who had crossed the Atlantic.

"Yes, I did!" the woman's husband answered. "Someone will be here. Don't worry so much!"

"Well, I don't want to have to take public transportation. I've heard the transit system often stops running."

"Look. There he is. His sign has our name on it. Come on."

They hurried off before Jessica could ask if Harry had heard something she hadn't about a possible shutdown in Paris. She tried to search the internet on her cell phone but couldn't find any mention of problems.

"Yes!" Jessica called out in joy when she finally confirmed from a fellow traveler, who gratefully spoke enough English to understand her question, that her arrival had not coincided with one of the innumerable episodes of *grèves*, or strikes, which seemed to endlessly plague the city. So at least Alain shouldn't have to contend with hours and hours of frustrating traffic snarls on the way over to the airport. He had insisted on meeting her there so that they could make the drive to central Paris together.

Jessica had managed to secure the short-term rental of a small apartment in a part of the city near the Parc Monceau. The lodgings were on the Boulevard de Courcelles in the seventeenth arrondissement. She was looking forward to enjoying the nearby gardens of the park and perhaps even finding time to take a few runs on its curved pathways. The apartment's owners, a married pair of lawyers who were currently vacationing in Switzerland, had assured her that the building's concierge, Madame Clair, would make sure she lacked for nothing.

Jessica had to admit that she was anxious about handling the Parisian apartment on her own, not even considering for a moment the difficult project Tom had faithfully entrusted to her. But she hadn't been able to resist the idea of living like a native, even if only for a short time. Besides, she had reckoned, her last two stays in hotels hadn't exactly turned out to be relaxing escapades. During the first stay in Montreal, she had been embroiled in the case of the death of her former mentor on top of Mount Royal, and in her next stay in Miami, she had helped solve the mystery of an elderly man's demise, at the same time facilitating the return of a piece of World War II–era artwork to its rightful owner. So she figured maybe this time a rental would bring her better luck for a chance at less sensationalism. At least it was worth a try.

She liked that the neighborhood she chose would allow her to walk to Musée Averi, which turned out to be just one of several private museums located in the area. She could imagine herself strolling the broad boulevards and avenues. She would revel in the beautiful architecture around her and soak up the local color. It would be her payback for being Tom's leg man in Paris. As of yet, she had no idea how much time she would need to spend at the museum or even if she would be successful at gaining entry to hidden areas off limits to an American tourist.

Jessica had told Alain she was coming and where she was staying and had given him a vague outline of what she had promised Tom she would do, but she had spared him several important details. She figured it would be a better plan to provide them to him when they were face-to-face and she would be able to make her case for his help more effectively. Now, here she was in Paris, once again on the lookout for the Canadian narcotics inspector's sturdy form among a crowd of people. Suddenly, over the heads of the travelers closest to her, she spotted him. He caught sight of her at the same time and was heading in her direction.

"Bonjour, Jessica. You made it," he said after giving her a hug and three alternating kisses on either side of her cheeks.

"And why wouldn't I have? Alain, you have no faith in me."

"Ah. Jessica, nothing has changed. You have remained the very image of a shrinking violet! Asking a question where none is necessary."

"I wasn't aware that you were familiar with that particular metaphor. I must say, I'm impressed. Anyway, Alain, thank you for meeting me. I overheard an American couple worrying about transportation, and their anxiety was contagious. I wasn't eager to get on-the-job training with the French transit system the instant I arrived here."

"I don't blame you. It's been awhile since I've been here myself, but I'm getting accustomed to the routine. And you will too. Is that all you have?" He looked down at her small rolling suitcase with an expression of disbelief at its diminutive size.

"I've learned from experience to travel light—even to Paris. Besides, what better excuse to buy Parisian couture than to run out of laundry while I'm here? Of course, I'll ignore all the glorious advertisements plastered on the airport walls … at least until we get to the city." She pointed to a particularly large one looming over their shoulders. It was a photograph of an American movie actress, no longer in the first blush of youth, hawking the designs of one of the many Parisian fashion houses with global reach. But somehow in Paris the picture seemed even more flattering than Jessica would have expected. And she took comfort in the thought that maybe the Paris air would also freshen up her own appearance a bit.

She hadn't thought to stop and check how she looked after getting off the plane, and now she wondered why, in heaven's name, she hadn't stopped to do so. Well, it was too late now. She wasn't going to pop into a ladies' room and take a look at herself in a mirror. It was just too obvious a maneuver.

"I have my car outside. Let's get going then," Alain said, pulling Jessica along steadily out of the concourse.

"Sounds like a plan," she said, only momentarily glancing back once more at the advertisement on the wall.

They left the airport terminal and then, after some minutes, a highway, and they were soon driving through the streets of Paris neighborhoods, which seemed to get more and more elegant the closer they got to central Paris as the suburbs transitioned to the very center of the city. The city was practically glistening that morning: beams of light bounced off dark, sloping, mansard roofs that encased the tops of the gracious buildings lining the streets.

There had been a recent rain, and the city smelled from it and almost tasted of it. Jessica pulled down the window on her side of the car, leaned her head out to catch the air, and took in the scents and sights around her. The remaining small pools of water, lingering from the fresh downpour, abutted the sidewalks and splashed up as the car turned the corners of streets and boulevards, nearly hitting her in the face. But she didn't mind. The roadways had been meticulously laid out so many years ago to create the more modern city she was now taking in. But the plan still worked, and she began to get a feel for its layout; she started to anticipate each new sight at each new intersection. Although it was hot and humid, the sky was now clear and vivid blue, with only an occasional white fluffy cloud breaking through and reminding her of the more temperamental weather that had just passed through the city.

They reached Avenue des Champs-Élysées, and Jessica was soon transfixed by the pageant of elegant boutiques and storefronts, interspersed with more eclectic offerings that greeted her all up and down the huge avenue. The large trees on either side of the street provided a green canopy of their own in front of the overhead signs of the shops. Her mind involuntarily began calculating the remaining free space left in her small suitcase to determine if it might accommodate at least a scarf or two to bring home with her—something to tie about her neck with abandon in any number of provocative arrangements. And she wondered for a moment if she hadn't shown too much bravado in thinking she could make do with her one piece of carry-on luggage, which she had bragged about to Alain.

Before she could finish her mental measurements, she looked in the other direction and caught sight of the massive Arc de Triomphe perched in the very center of Place Charles de Gaulle, and all thoughts of purchases quickly flew out of her mind. The arch reminded her of a large bird of prey, ready to consume all comers, as it loomed over the intersecting roads that were arranged like the spokes of a wheel at its base. Cars circled around it in a dizzying roundabout, and she had even more respect for her companion's excellent driving skills as he darted through the traffic.

From there, Alain turned the car around a couple of times until Jessica realized they were now driving down the length of Boulevard de Courcelles, where her rental apartment was located. She tried to scan the buildings for one that bore any resemblance to the façade that had been posted on the internet when she had first made the rental arrangements. Finally, she saw it. There it was.

Alain stopped the car in front of a building, which was part of the unified row of similar buildings lining the boulevard. Jessica peered out of the window to get a better look at what was to be her temporary home for the length of her stay in Paris. The building was clearly what the French called an *immeuble Haussmanien*. It was five floors of massive cut stone blocks with black, wrought iron balconies and elaborate cut stonework around the windows. She knew her apartment was on what the listing had referred to as the fourth floor, although Americans would consider it the fifth floor, and she tried in vain to pinpoint which of the many windows might be part of it as she eagerly scanned the outline of the building for any clues.

"Alain, would you mind leaving me off here?" she said. "I think I want to deal with Madame Clair on my own—she's the concierge—and to get settled in all by myself. I shouldn't be long, and I can meet you anywhere you like as soon as I'm done. To be honest, I would love a cup of good, strong French coffee to give me a jolt and get me going again. But I want to take the first stab at handling Parisian life on my own." She also thought that finally this was her chance to freshen up and repair whatever she needed to in her appearance. Oh, she was subtle, wasn't she?

"That's a good idea. You look like you could use some caffeine."

"Do I look that bad?"

"No, not at all. You look great. Just tired. That's all."

"Thanks. That makes me feel better. It's good to be appreciated."

"You know I do. I'm just a man of few words."

"That I know. And I like your style."

They both got out of the car, and Alain handed her the suitcase out of the back. Then he said, "Far be it from me to interfere with your introduction to Madame Clair, who I'm sure is a redoubtable woman. Let's just hope she hasn't retired and been replaced by a cleaning company. That's often the case in Paris, unfortunately. Anyway, I'll park the car, and when you're done, you'll find me at an outdoor table at the café on Rue du Faubourg Saint-Honoré. You can't miss it." He pointed over his shoulder in the general direction she would need to go when she was ready to meet him, and then he got back into the car.

As soon as he drove away, Jessica, with her suitcase in tow, turned away from the road and pushed open the heavy, wooden double doors of the building, entered the vestibule, and was immediately gratified to see a diminutive cage-like elevator inside. Although the abutting well-worn stairs to the upper floors looked shallow and easy to climb, Jessica knew that without the tiny metal contraption to help her up to her floor, she would soon tire of at least one aspect of the local color—that of climbing up and down innumerable stairs.

"Bonjour. Bonjour," Jessica called out tentatively, looking around her for the concierge's apartment that she had been informed still existed in this particular setup.

"Bonjour," she quickly heard back. A tiny elderly woman, no bigger than a child, dressed impeccably in a white bouclé suit, soon greeted her from a doorway off to the side of the lobby. The miniscule size of the woman, as well as the absence of any color to her suit, which didn't have a speck of dust on it, seemed to support Alain's prescient assumption that this building supplemented its needed physical labors with the help of a cleaning service. The woman emerged from the *loge de concierge* and came over to Jessica with a step that was sprightlier than should have been associated with the woman's obviously advanced age.

"*Vous êtes Madame Clair?*" Jessica asked in her rudimentary French, hoping her pronunciation of the simple greeting was adequate.

"*Oui. Oui. Je suis Clair Laforêt.* You are Jessica Shepard, are you not?"

Jessica breathed a sigh of relief, realizing the woman's English was good and she didn't appear to have any reluctance at conversing with her in English. She began appraising Jessica, studying her up and down with the knowing eyes of someone who was likely watchman and emotional confidant for the building's many apartment owners.

"Yes, I am. I'm the one subletting the apartment on the fourth floor."

"I know all about it. That's *mon travail*, yes? I have the key. Let me go and get it, and I'll take you inside right now. I was told to expect you. And you must be very tired after your long trip. I can see that."

Again, it ran through Jessica's mind that the thing she needed most was a mirror.

A few minutes later, Madame Clair opened the door to a light-filled apartment with highly polished parquet floors and ornamented plaster walls. It had high ceilings and appeared to be in fairly good condition, although it showed some obvious signs of age. But Jessica was gratified to see that fresh, fragrant flowers had been placed in a few vases that were scattered about the apartment. The scent of the flowers mingled with the smell of vinegar, which had clearly been used to meticulously clean the apartment for her expected arrival. Madame Clair knew her *travail*. It was an auspicious welcome, and Jessica was immediately enamored by her new accommodations.

The concierge then began to proudly give Jessica the personal tour. "Like most Paris apartments that haven't been aggressively renovated to modern tastes, the kitchen is in the back at the end of this hallway."

As they visited each room in turn—the living room, the bedroom, the bathroom, and finally the tiny kitchen, which looked out onto a pretty little garden out back—she pointed at each of them, one by one, with delicate hands laced with small blue veins evident through her fragile, crinkly skin. "Unfortunately, there is no air-conditioning. But there is the bathroom with shower that I showed you; they did that for the Americans they sublet to." She smiled and handed Jessica the heavy key, demonstrating that the tour had finally reached its conclusion.

"It's perfect. I'm glad everything is just the way it is. It's very charming. I'm sure I'll feel right at home here. Thank you."

"Ah," Madame Clair sighed deeply and smiled. "That is what is so often said to me when I let the renters in to see *des appartements*. But I must go now. I have so much to do. Remember, I'm on the first floor should you need anything. If you like, I will be happy to point out who in the building you should cultivate as *amis* and who you should avoid. *Au revoir.*"

Jessica left her new residence and quickly walked toward her rendezvous with Alain, content in the fact that she had situated herself into her apartment with relative ease. She was half-tempted to take a short detour and try to scout out the Musée

Averi, at least from the outside. But she knew any further delay would most likely irritate Alain, and the last thing she needed to do at this time was antagonize him. She needed his help, and she knew she was going to be pushing his good nature to the limits with this latest request. She also knew that she had no choice. She just had to do all she could to help Tom and his sister get to the bottom of what had happened to Lucy and what had caused Lucy so much unhappiness.

Jessica came to Place des Ternes and made a sharp left to Rue du Faubourg Saint-Honoré. She started scouting out the patrons who were seated in front of the café where Alain told her he would be waiting. She quickly spotted him.

"Here I am again," she said, walking over to his table and sitting down beside him in a metal chair. Sitting outside together this way evoked a memory that was often in her thoughts. It suddenly reminded her of another summer when she had first met Alain and they had shared an outdoor table at a café in Montreal.

At that time, they had not yet learned to understand each other as well as they did now. Then he had needed her assistance with what turned out to be a murder case. So much had happened since then, and their relationship had changed so much. Inexplicably and for a moment, a slight chill passed over her, and she wondered what it could mean. It was warm outside, and the sun was shining and striking the table between them with its comforting rays. She hoped that if it was a short spasm of anxiety, it didn't presage anything significant but just her trepidation at having to request such a big favor of him. Or, perhaps, she thought pushing the feeling away, it was just the natural effect of jet lag after her long flight from home.

"How did it go? Are you all settled in?" he asked.

"Reasonably so."

"So you managed. How was Madame Clair?"

"Straight out of a French novel. Believe it or not, the typical Parisian concierge—or at least the one I would expect her to be—exquisitely garbed, of course."

"Excellent. I'm gratified to hear that Paris hasn't disappointed you."

"No—at least not yet. Did you wait to order?" Jessica assessed the empty tabletop in front of him. "You shouldn't have. I might have been longer if Madame Clair hadn't been so efficient. I hope I look a little better?" Jessica smoothed her hair, which she had already brushed out several times before the long mirror in her new bedroom.

"You look much improved."

"Thank you."

"You're welcome. Anyway, I was happy to wait for you. It's a beautiful day. The waiter knows to bring two coffees once you arrive." No sooner was that said than the drinks were placed in front of them. Alain looked at her face closely and then said, "So, Jessica, tell me what I'm letting myself in for this time. I can only imagine what you have up your sleeve. You are in luck that I'm now here strictly as a vacationer while I keep an eye on my daughter for her mother while Josephine and Claude … You remember I told you that's my ex-wife's new husband. Anyway, they're out of town. So my time is now relatively free except for what Odette needs. I'm all yours otherwise, which isn't often the case."

"How is it going with Odette, by the way? Are you getting along okay? The teenage years can be a difficult time, although from what you've told me, I can't imagine you having any major problems."

"It's been going very well, as a matter of fact. Odette's matured a good deal since we last spent so much time together, and that's been helpful. I'm very proud of how she's handling the responsibility of interning at Musée Averi. It can only help her continue to excel in her lycée. I'm proud to say that she's a smart girl and a very conscientious student at that. It's really quite remarkable when you come to think about it."

"I'm sure you're very proud of her, Alain. You know, it is the very circumstance of her interning at Musée Averi that is such an amazing coincidence."

"In what way, might I ask?"

Jessica could see him involuntarily tense up his body. It was unusual for him. He so rarely gave any outward hint of his emotions, and she knew it was because she had crossed an invisible line between them in mentioning his daughter the way she just had. She decided she would have to tread softly, which she also considered appropriate.

"Well, remember I mentioned that an additional reason for my coming to Paris was to help out my friend, Tom Martine, and his sister Lucy?"

"Yes," he replied curtly, allowing her no easy out except for her to continue with her explanation.

She could sense the continued tensing of his musculature, and it made her think of a dog raising its haunches, ears, and tail before it is ready to pounce to protect its young.

"I don't want to get into details about Lucy's medical condition, although I do want to say that she's had a rough time of it," Jessica continued.

"I'm sorry about that."

"Thank you. Anyway, you see, I promised Tom that I'd do my best to help him find out anything I could about Frédéric Averi. You remember I said that he's the man behind the company that performed a genetic test for her that Tom wasn't happy with. I know I didn't go into much detail. I didn't feel I ought to."

"I do remember what you told me."

"Well, it's probably obvious to you that Averi's a very rich and powerful man here with many different businesses around the globe. He apparently owns a château in the French countryside, which he's parlaying into a major tourist attraction. He also owns a private art museum. Tom has created quite an extensive dossier on him that he shared with me. Averi's into artificial intelligence, machine-learning applications, delivery robots, and self-driving cars, among other things. He seems to have his finger in every pot. Well, one of his other technological interests has been genetics. His business has a venture capital arm that invested heavily in the genetic testing lab that Lucy happened to use, and it turns out that it might not have been as ready for market as it should have been. At least, that's Tom's take on it."

"And Tom thinks that Averi might have put profits over performance. Is that what you're driving at?"

"Exactly so. You understand me perfectly."

"So why isn't Tom here doing the legwork for himself? He's a big boy. I wouldn't think he would need you to do his homework for him."

"Alain, he's having to handle Lucy at the moment. It's not as easy as you make it sound. You have to understand that as well." Jessica snapped at him before realizing he was making a valid point. She knew she must not allow any further defensiveness to creep into her voice. It wouldn't help her by any means. It was the very worst way to deal with Alain.

They had always dealt with each other as intellectual equals. She knew that her analytical brain was one of the things he most respected her for. "Look. You can't have failed to connect the dots: Frédéric Averi, Musée Averi, Odette having an internship at the very art museum Averi owns. You couldn't make this any easier if it were handed to us on a plate."

"*Us* did you say?"

"Yes, of course I said *us*. We've been a team, Alain, ever since I've known you, and we always will be. You know that. We almost *gel*."

She could see the tension in his large body finally begin to relax. She had handled it just the right way. But then the tension was replaced by a good deal of skepticism, which virtually spread across his earnest face.

"Jessica, I don't want to involve Odette in anything that would put her in any harm, in any way. You should *know* that!"

"Of course not, and I wouldn't want that either. Just talk to her, Alain. All she would need to do is help us get inside the museum—into places we otherwise wouldn't be able to get to and meet insiders we otherwise wouldn't be able to meet. Use your imagination. This is your specialty, not mine!"

Jessica finished speaking with a flourish and almost upset the good strong cup of French coffee that was still sitting untouched in its china cup and saucer on the small bistro table between them. She realized she had become impassioned, which was probably not the best way to get over Alain's persisting reluctance to involve his daughter in his work, even if it was at her behest.

But she also knew from everything that she had heard about Odette previously, and from what Alain had just added, that the teenager was extremely bright and eager to be involved in her father's life, especially his professional life. At one time, Alain had even hinted at Odette considering a career in detective work. Jessica knew she was convincing herself mentally, as well as Alain verbally, as to the benefits of her plan.

Again, unlike his usual inscrutability, she could almost see
him mentally weighing the options of her proposition over and
over in his mind. Then at last he said, "Very well. This is what
I'll do and only what I'll do: I will talk to Odette and determine
her level of agreement with involvement in this escapade of
yours. In the meantime, you stay out of trouble."

"What possible *trouble* would I get into?" Jessica asked, her
eyebrows rising in mock surprise, satisfied in having obtained
her difficult objective.

"You know what I mean. Just lie low for now. Take in some
of the Parisian sights. Be a typical American tourist, at least
until you hear back from me. As soon as I get Odette's sign-off
on this, we'll see how best to deal with Musée Averi."

Jessica left Alain at the café after finally finishing her stone-cold
coffee. She was encouraged by his parting words. She was fairly
confident that his daughter would be willing to help them. She
just had a feeling about it. With Alain's cooperation assured
and Odette's all but guaranteed, Jessica decided she would take
his advice and scout out the local landscape on her own. Alain
knew her so well. A chance to explore her new surroundings
was just what she thrived on and what would allow her to wait
out the hours before any further action could be taken. She decided she would take her time and meander through the small
side streets of the city toward the obvious choice: to march up
Avenue des Champs-Élysées to the Arc de Triomphe, a reasonable first stop for any new visitor to the city. Hadn't Alain
instructed her to play the tourist?

She zigzagged through streets that caught her eye and stared
into the shop windows that enticed her: one was selling all sorts

of delectable looking white, yellow, and orange cheeses punctured by little signs with descriptive names on them, and another held behind its windows a variety of chocolate bonbons she was certain would melt in her mouth. Reinvigorated by the coffee she had just imbibed, she resisted the temptation to sample either the cheeses or the chocolates, and she plowed on, proud in her ability to resist such oral delicacies. The selections and arrangements were all so different from what she was accustomed to back at home that it hadn't been easy. Finally, fearful she would end up becoming hopelessly lost and never be able to find her way back, she managed to relocate more recognizable streets and was soon walking up one of them to her initial goal—the Avenue des Champs-Élysées.

At that time of day, the broad avenue was virtually teeming with pedestrians of all ages and sizes strolling on the sidewalks, and cars were bumper-to-bumper in the street between the surrounding pavements. As she joined the flock of people moving together up the avenue, a sense of exhilaration, which she had first experienced upon her arrival at the airport earlier that day, again flooded over her and gave her even more momentum, propelling her forward ever faster. The sights and sounds of the city were even closer around her, and she was totally taken in by them.

At the hub of the web of twelve avenues diverging in a circle from Place Charles de Gaulle, she again saw the large arch rising up ahead of her into the blue sky. She went down and then up through the metro underpasses to get to the arch, while at the same time avoiding being an American casualty of the Parisian traffic relentlessly circling the arch. A few minutes later success was at hand, and she exited at the arch's very base.

Surprised by her lack of fatigue after the recent plane trip and the fact that she hadn't stopped walking since she had left

Alain at the café, she decided to climb the 284 steps to the top terrace. She wanted to see the city laid out below from the height of the top of the arch above. She bought her ticket and handed it to the guard before starting to climb, ignoring his subtle smile, which he clearly flashed to each new tourist, probably to indicate that the climb wouldn't be that easy—as if the number of steps to the top hadn't already made that obvious. Not to be discouraged by his possible lack of confidence in her physical reserves, she decided to resolutely press on.

Thank you very much! she thought to herself.

Making her way up the well-trodden stone steps that circled tightly around and around level by level in the narrow stairway, Jessica couldn't help but once again appreciate the cage-like contraption installed in Madame Clair's building. Refusing to give up in her heroic quest, she was finally rewarded by seeing the light up ahead of her. She then exited the stairway at the top, led on by an enthusiastic group of Japanese tourists as eager as she for a glimpse and breath of open air and the promised view from the top.

Jessica was not disappointed as she looked out over the ledge of the terrace of the arch. The teeming crowds on the broad avenues she had been a part of just minutes before were now merely specks, spread out below her like ants on a log. The web of avenues radiating out from the arch was even more dramatic when viewed from that height. The roofs of the buildings and the greenery of the trees above the people below gave her a sense of the pulse of the city as they all meshed together in one panoramic image. The payoff had been worth the effort and price of the ticket.

Following the perimeter of the arch from corner to corner, guided by representative maps intermittently provided to the many visitors, she finally reached the side with the best view of the Eiffel Tower. She forgave herself the cliché of acting like a tourist. Hadn't Alain said it was the thing to do? She felt one more frisson of excitement course through her when she spotted it, despite Guy de Maupassant's derision, as the author had reportedly eaten lunch every day at its base because it was the only place in Paris he wouldn't have to see it. Well, she liked it. The engineering masterpiece of iron caught her fancy as she saw, even from the great distance, its powerful and majestic lines rise up in elegant curves. It was like a bridge stacked up in the air instead of lying on its side. The effect was dramatic.

But as she followed the tower's length up in the air to pierce the blue sky above, the tower seemed like more of a totem than a tourist spot, willing her to remember her purpose for crossing the Atlantic to come to this beautiful city. Standing there, she silently vowed that she would do her best to find out anything and everything she could about Frédéric Averi in order to help Tom and Lucy. But for now, she would await Alain's green light and hope that Musée Averi and Odette would provide the first goalpost for her to reach.

3

Odette Comes Through

Jessica and Alain waited in front of the doors of Musée Averi. The museum was situated in such a way so that the elegant mansion that housed its collection seemed totally divorced from the hustle and bustle of the vibrant city surrounding it. The large cobblestone courtyard in which they now stood provided the best view of the building, which was replete with and embellished by innumerable floor-to-ceiling windows on its facade. The building had multiple balustraded terraces rising above the courtyard. They served to add even more grandeur to the exterior of the mansion, and Jessica could envision herself in another time, dressed in elegant garb and hanging over any one of them to meet new guests arriving in horse-drawn carriages, the clip-clop of the horses' hooves echoing against the cobblestones.

As the air in the courtyard was redolent of fragrant smells emanating from ornamental trees in large planters that dotted the cobblestoned entrance with almost geometric precision, Jessica sniffed the air in appreciation of their delicious scents as they waited for entrance to the museum.

"Cozy little place, isn't it?" Jessica asked.

"To say the least," Alain said. "Odette will come out and

bring us inside herself. I said I would text her when we got here." He took his cell phone out of the inner pocket of his jacket and punched in the communication to his daughter.

"Alain, I hope you told Odette how grateful I am that she agreed to get us inside this way. How much did you tell her?"

"Only what she needed to know to get us into the areas that might hold some answers for us. But she obviously knows there's more than I've let on. I told you she's smart. Anyway, I'm still not sure how much we'll be able to find out. She's only a summer intern, after all. But maybe we'll be able to make some helpful connections inside. Let's see what happens. We'll only know what the setup is once we get there."

Several minutes later, a young girl, who Jessica thought looked exactly like she had at sixteen years of age, exited the building and came over to them. She was small in stature and extremely pretty, with long brown hair and olive coloring. She was wearing an obviously borrowed Musée Averi blazer that was much too large for her. The generous size of the jacket required her to roll back the sleeves several times over her small wrists. But the exposed silk lining failed to give Odette a casual look because of the impressive silver-threaded Musée Averi insignia that was embroidered over her left breast pocket. The insignia matched exactly the one emblazoned on the plaque positioned over the entranceway of the museum.

But no formality of any kind could be found in the delighted smile the young girl flashed at her father as he leaned over to plant kisses on either side of his daughter's cheeks. Any hint of concern Jessica might have had about Odette's possible reluctance to help them gain entry to the museum's more private spaces, despite Alain's assurances, flew out of her head as she witnessed the tenderness of the father-daughter greeting that morning. In an instant, Jessica knew Odette would do anything to help them. Odette's verbal confirmation of the fact came immediately after.

"Bonjour, Jessica. It is so nice to meet you. Papa has enlisted me in the caper, and I am happy to show you whatever I can. I told Mason Henri—he's supervising me for the summer—that my father and a friend of his from America want to see the museum with me as their guide, and he was fine with it. Mason's great. You'll see."

Jessica was quickly impressed by Odette's excellent command of English, especially in one so young; she spoke it easily, without a hint of a French accent. Jessica wondered if it was due to the girl's probable facility with the global internet, not to mention her father's usual North American residence in Canada, where she was likely to have visited and been more exposed to both French and English speakers.

"Thank you, Odette. I really appreciate your willingness to help us. Your father has been telling me what an excellent student you are, and we're both excited to see where you are working."

Odette immediately took charge and led them through the entrance so that Jessica got her first glimpse of the interior of the museum. It seemed to her to be more reminiscent of an exquisite private residence than a museum: small, intimate living spaces gave way to each other through hallways of highly polished marble floors. One after another, the rooms provided a private peek at what it must be like to live in elegant good taste, unconstrained by impingement of tight finances. The walls were hung with large classical paintings set in gilded frames, whose opulence of subject matter was only surpassed by the luxury of the accompanying furnishings in each room. Jessica could not help but begin to calculate the value of each room's artistic contents, and the maneuver helped confirm her already formed impression of Averi's apparent wealth—at least in terms of his more material assets.

At last, the three of them, with Odette still in the lead, went through a door marked *Département Administratif.* It led into the more private area of the museum and the part that they would presumably never have had access to without Odette's acquiescence to Jessica's plan. Behind the door lay a short corridor with business offices on either side of the hallway.

"Come this way," Odette said. She confidently pointed ahead and then opened the door of the first room they came to and ushered them inside.

The room was an office in which two desks had been arranged, one in front of the other. Each had a large computer terminal upon it. Odette's desk was closer to the door, and at a slightly larger desk behind it, positioned under a back window, sat a young man who looked to be about thirty years in age. He had a face that was notable for thick, dark brown eyebrows, which almost met each other in the center of his brow; they were raised over black, round-framed glasses, and together they gave him an appearance that reminded Jessica of a serious owl. He was staring intently at his computer screen with a slight frown that made the convergence of his two eyebrows even more noticeable. But when he saw that Jessica and Alain had entered the room, he immediately shut off his computer, rose from his chair, and came over politely to greet Odette's new guests.

"Bonjour," he said, looking quizzically at his young coworker as he appraised Jessica and Alain, seemingly unsure how best to formally address the new arrivals.

"Mason, this is my papa and the friend of his I told you about," Odette said in English, clearly signifying that any further conversation had best be conducted in the native tongue of her father's companion. "Monsieur Henri is cataloguing the collection of art and furnishings in the museum. He's been wonderful at helping me to learn as much as I can."

"Cataloguing the collection of a museum such as this must be quite an endeavor if what we passed so far is any sample of its size," Jessica offered, looking encouragingly at the young man who seemed to positively reek of awkward shyness. Jessica had not envisioned him exactly so based on Odette's enthusiastic commentary. She suddenly realized that perhaps Alain had been correct, and this young man and a summer intern would be unlikely to be able to provide much helpful information for Tom Martine's needs. On the other hand, one never knew where any lead would take one, and it was all they had at present to work with. "I imagine Frédéric Averi must be a man of some means to have created a museum such as this on his own."

Mason momentarily hesitated before speaking, as though weighing how best he should respond to the obvious, before saying, "Yes. He is."

Suddenly, his former reticence seemed to disappear, and he began speaking with such animation that Jessica could see, for just a moment, a little of what Odette had obviously already noted about her coworker.

"I have been working for many months to create a complete record and have only just scratched the surface of all that is here. I haven't even begun to think of the next phase of my employ-ment, which will be to catalogue the items at the château." He shook his head slightly as though to emphasize the enormity of the projects ahead of him. "That will be an even more ex-tensive undertaking. But there I hope to have the assistance of Monsieur Averi's assistant, Monsieur Dom Roberts. He has been in Monsieur Averi's employ for many years and knows the château inside and out. So it won't be all on my shoulders alone."

Despite the modesty of his speech, Jessica could now also catch a hint of Mason's obvious pride in his own work by the gleam in his eyes and the satisfied smile that crossed his lips as he spoke; they added to the animation in his voice. The signs seemed to contradict the content of his modest words.

"I hope that Odette has been contributing positively to your effort," Alain said.

"Yes, she has, and I am confident she will continue to do so." He smiled, this time more broadly in Odette's direction.

Jessica could palpably sense a connection between the two young people.

"Odette mentioned that she wishes to give you both a private tour of the museum. Why don't you let her show you the upper gallery first? That's where what I think are the most precious items are housed." Mason turned back to Odette and continued, "I still have several hours of work here before I break, so it's probably best if you take them up there on your own. You know what to show them, I think." He smiled at her again.

With the dismissal, Odette took her cue. She led her father and Jessica back out of the office she was sharing with Mason, through the administrative hallway, and on to the public part of the museum they had first seen. From there, the group ascended a large marble staircase. It was a magnificent structure that wound around itself in a serpentine curve and on up to the upper floor. Jessica marveled at the mastery of its construction that would allow such a monumental work of heavy marble to seemingly float in the air by its own support and not come crashing down upon itself into pieces on the floor below.

Once at the top of the staircase, they were soon navigating around an extensive quadrangular minstrels' gallery, whose walls were covered with large paintings, as had been the ones on the ground floor. From the look of the paintings, Jessica guessed that each piece of art was individually worth in the hundreds of thousands, if not millions, of dollars or even euros. It seemed that Monsieur Averi had a particular fondness for Renaissance art as well as for the old Dutch masters; both genres formed the bulk of the paintings they saw in the gallery. But a few items from later periods were also represented there, although not as extensively as the others. It seemed that nothing was to be overlooked when it came to acquisitions for Musée Averi, and Jessica assumed for Frédéric Averi.

Jessica slowly walked around the perimeter of the generous space, taking in the superb brushstrokes of each painting in turn. It was clear, even to her relatively inexpert eye, that they all were of extremely high quality, and she recognized many of the names of the painters, although some she did not. As she went around the quadrangle, she was cognizant of the need to keep very close to the walls of the gallery because the floored area was relatively narrow and the wooden balustrades surrounding the open space in the middle were not particularly bulky and were delicately carved. She had no wish to put significant pressure on them with a careless wrist or test their intrinsic strength at preventing her from falling far to the marble floor below. It was quite a drop.

Once they had made a full circuit around the corners of the gallery, Odette led them farther through to another series of small rooms of an even more intimate nature than the ones they had already seen. These rooms seemed to give the impression that they were those that would only be allowed to be visualized by special guests. And Jessica was encouraged by the fact that Mason Henri had directed Odette to take them to see them first; in each of them were paintings, finely woven tapestries, and alabaster statuaries.

They found a corner of one of the better lit rooms where

there was a bench situated directly across from a particularly arresting painting. It was about four feet from top to bottom and six feet across and set in a heavy back frame—so different from the delicately gilded frames containing many of the other paintings in the museum. The subject of the tableau was of a group of men and women dressed in period costumes and seated around a table in a tavern. Wine was flowing in the tavern and evidently being imbibed by the tavern patrons from the look of the rosy hues painted on their cheeks, and it was evident that ribaldry was on the menu. But at the same time, there were ironic touches painted into the scene, and the irony of their situation hit Jessica as she thought about whether Odette would be able to direct them in any meaningful investigative direction. So the bench seemed an appropriate setting for any discussion between the three of them.

Jessica decided to plunge right in. "Odette, how much have you learned so far about the museum's owner, Frédéric Averi?"

"Frédéric Averi? Let me think. Frédéric Averi only rarely comes by the museum to see how things are going. So what I've learned about him so far has only come to me secondhand. I've asked Mason about him, and Mason said it's really Dom Roberts, whom he mentioned to you, who's responsible for most of the museum's day-to-day operations. Dom Roberts is not formally the director of the museum—at least not for now, although maybe he wants to be. I think Mason said at this time he's M. Averi's general assistant. But from what Mason's told me about him, he seems to function as more than an assistant: M. Roberts calls a lot of the shots around here. I haven't met him yet either, but Mason says he comes by from time to time, so I probably will soon. I just need more time."

Jessica was again impressed by Odette's maturity and guessed that Alain had been right. *This girl probably does realize*

more than her father let her in on. She is a detective's daughter,
after all. "I guess Averi's busy with all his investments and
needs someone to delegate the running of the museum and
the château. That doesn't seem that unusual, does it, Alain?"
Jessica asked, looking to him for confirmation.

"Not necessarily. Of course, delegation does have its own
inherent risks. Odette, how long has Mason been working on
this cataloging project that he mentioned? How much do you
know about it? And how much do you know about him? He
seems to be our best source of information. If he's cataloging
items, he's likely to have some access to financial figures—at
least as they pertain to the museum, although less likely to
other holdings."

"Papa, Mason's great. He works night and day. And he
never treats me like a child."

Jessica observed Alain's eyebrows go up slightly as he listened to his daughter speak with some defensiveness about her
current mentor. It was clear that Odette was at that difficult
age that straddled childhood and adulthood. Her loyalties to
her father's wishes and to her own sense of independence were
clearly being forced to struggle against each other. So perhaps
what Jessica was requesting of father and daughter in her attempt to help Tom and Lucy would be an excellent way to help
build that necessary bridge for Odette, as well as a balance
between the two opposing forces. She would need to come over
that bridge. The thought helped to relieve some of Jessica's
discomfort about imposing upon Alain and Odette; it was still
nagging at her, and anything that helped Jessica come to terms
with her own competing needs was welcome to her.

Odette waited a minute to let her words sink in as Jessica's
own thoughts were swirling around her head, and then Odette
said, "Mason is not only cataloguing all the art and furnishings

but is helping value them as well. He says these items are not just paintings and furniture but national treasures that must be preserved and insured." Odette concluded her impassioned speech, and for the first time that Jessica had observed her, she seemed irritated with the adults around her. Maybe crossing that bridge wouldn't be so easy.

"Alain, I think we've kept Odette from her internship duties long enough," Jessica said, breaking in diplomatically. "Odette, it was fabulous to meet you. I'm sure this is a great experience. Are you considering a career in art rather than your father's own line of detective work?"

Jessica obviously had succeeded in redirecting the young girl's thoughts away from any controversy because Odette immediately brightened up and said cryptically, "Maybe. We'll see."

"Well, you're certainly working in more pleasant surroundings than I'm used to," Alain added, following Jessica's diplomatic lead. "I'll see you at home tonight, Odette. Now Jessica and I will let you get back to work."

4

Mason Henri's Problem

After escorting her father and Jessica out of the museum and deciding it was time to concentrate on her own issues rather than that of her father and his so-called friend, Odette left the gallery and headed back down the marble staircase.

As she went down the stairs, she felt a little troubled. She hoped she hadn't been rude before they had left so abruptly. She had agreed to help and had been excited by the prospect of being a part of her father's life that she was rarely let in on. But at the same time, she couldn't help but feel a touch of resentment swell up inside her. Her mother and stepfather, Claude, were away, and this was the time she was to spend with Papa. And she wanted him to see her as grown up, which she knew he did at many times. But she also knew that, at others, he still saw her as his little girl.

She had thought helping him would be a chance to be important in his life, and she knew she was. But she also had a little sense of guilt about it, especially as this summer internship was important to her. Besides, she really liked Mason. As she had told her Papa, Mason didn't treat her like a child. Well, maybe she hadn't been rude after all, just setting her own boundaries. She had a right to, didn't she?

Odette returned to the administrative office, and there was Mason, fixed in position in front of his computer as usual.

"You're back," he said, looking up at her. Noticing that she was now alone, he switched back to conversing in the casual French they used with each other. "Did they enjoy the upper gallery?"

"Yes, they did. Thanks for suggesting it. Did you even take a break in all the time I was showing it to them?"

"No, not really. I didn't realize how long I've been working; I lost track of time while you were gone. But I found a few items that bothered me, and I've been so focused on them and trying to figure out some of the valuations that just don't make sense that I didn't notice the time fly by."

"The valuations? What do you mean? In what way are they bothering you? For insurance purposes, you mean?"

"For that and for some of the sales that have taken place. Look. Don't let it get around, but digging a little deeper into this has been kind of a pet project of my own. I wasn't yet ready to share all that I've been looking at up the chain of command."

"You're so dedicated, Mason. Are you going to discuss what you found with Monsieur Roberts when he next comes by?"

"No. Still not just yet. I want to make sure I haven't made any silly errors. That's all. I don't want to look like a fool in front of him."

Odette knew one of Mason's failings was his lack of confidence. She could see him studying her face, and she hoped she looked honestly concerned about him; she knew she was very mature for her age, but she was still just a teenager after all. Maybe he wasn't sure how much he could use her as a sounding board for his own insecurities.

She tried to read his thoughts because perhaps he wasn't aware that his lack of self-assurance was so obvious to others and then asked, "Then is there anyone else you can show the figures to?"

He waited a minute before responding. "Yes. There is now that I think about it. Remember Jacques Charles?"

"No, I don't. Not really."

"Yes, you do. He was here some time back ... an older man. He wore such a formal suit and a tie even though it was very hot that day. You mentioned it after he left, and we laughed about it. He used to do some of this work under contract before I started here. He knows Dom better than I do. I think I'll run some of my questions by him first ... just to make sure I'm not being foolish, especially if eventually I do go to Dom about them. And if I haven't made any errors, at least Jacques can give me a few ideas about how best to raise my concerns so I don't step on anyone's toes. He's sure to know more about that than I do."

"That sounds like a good idea. Why don't you do that. Do you feel better about it?"

"I think so. Anyway, enough about this for now. On your tour did you stop by the restaurant and get anything to eat?" Mason said.

She could tell he was definitely feeling better as he stood up and shut down his computer. His brow was no longer so furrowed in concern.

"No. We didn't," Odette said.

"Well, are you hungry now?"

"Yes. I'm practically starving."

"Good. Let's take that break and get something to eat. This can wait for now. The numbers aren't going away anytime soon, and I can deal with them later."

Mason left the RER Station Luxembourg on Boulevard St. Michel and headed toward Place du Panthéon in the Latin Quarter, near where Jacques Charles now ran a rare books shop. The area was filled with students attending the Sorbonne, and they seemed to fill the street at every corner. Some scurried past him on their way to classes; others strolled about more leisurely, obviously determined to laze in the nearby gardens or partake of refreshments at a café or eatery in the neighborhood.

But at the moment, Mason was not interested in the surroundings around him—no matter how pleasant. He was preoccupied with the papers he carried in his backpack. It was the *sac* that had served him faithfully for many years. He had taken the bag from the usual position he wore it, behind him, and had held it closely to his breast throughout the train ride here, as if it were a very delicate infant he wished to protect from harm. Now as he walked quickly toward Jacques's shop, the bag hung over his right shoulder. He wanted to be able to constantly see it through the corner of his eye as he marched about the hilltop to his goal.

His plan was to consult with the older man who had been his predecessor in employment at Musée Averi. Mason had always been good with numbers, and he knew in his heart that something was wrong with the figures he had found while cataloguing the museum's diverse holdings. But as certain in his own mind as he was, his lack of self-confidence kept reasserting itself, despite his many valiant attempts to suppress it, and he needed the assurance that Jacques's agreement with his suspicions would give him.

Mason spotted the wooden door frame of the shop with Jacques Charles listed as *libraire* in the window; the lights were on, and he let out a sigh of relief. It had been some time since he had visited Jacques, and part of the younger man was afraid that the older one might have decamped on vacation for some out-of-the-way environs away from Paris without leaving any way for Mason to reach him. He was happy to find, at least, that one fear hadn't materialized. He pulled open the heavy glass door of the entrance and was soon comforted by the pleasant twinkling sound of the bells overhead that rang out as he went inside. The sound seemed to him like the first few musical bars of an orchestra that was just beginning to play a familiar piece; when those notes hit his ears, it was as if they were leading him on in the right direction. He just knew it.

The shop itself was small, but it was crammed full of stacks of books of all varieties, both large and small. They lined the old wooden shelves running from floor to ceiling all around the perimeter of the store. In the middle of the store, other stacks of books that were too plentiful to fill the already crowded shelves were randomly arranged in neat piles on a few wooden counters. On one of the counters there was an old brass register, whose golden surfaces had been dulled by years of scrubbing, and black streaks of tarnish eroded some of the beauty of the antique object. Mason was momentarily distracted by it, and he wondered if it still worked or had been left there over the years for sentimental reasons. Even in its faded form, it somehow reminded him of the continuity over time of creative artifacts and of the importance of considering their intrinsic value. He was awoken from his thoughts by Jacques himself, who suddenly appeared to him from the recesses of the back of the store.

"Bonjour mon ami," the elder man said, speaking in French to the young man who had assumed his prior responsibilities. "So what brings you to my shop? Are you looking for a particular book that I may help you find?"

The shopkeeper was short of stature, although from the curvature of his back there was the suggestion that his height had been somewhat compromised by his advancing years; the kyphosis was noticeable even through the dark suit he wore. His attire was consistent with Mason's memory of the preferred conservative style of dress that he always seemed to wear. There was not a wrinkle upon him, and his suit jacket was in place, despite the lack of air-conditioning in the shop. Everything was just as Mason remembered. For a moment, it made Mason think of his father, who was no longer around but who had also clung to the formality in dress of the prior era. Somehow the comparison comforted Mason, and he felt his confidence growing in approaching Jacques for assistance.

"Bonjour, Jacques. I'm glad I found you in."

"But my friend, where else would you find me these days, now that I have relinquished to your capable and younger hands my former duties at M. Averi's museum? I am always here among my good friends—my books. I am no longer a young man like yourself, no doubt eager to be with your friends rather than piles of books. That is why I am surprised but happy to see you today. So what may I do for you?"

Mason could detect no trace of bitterness in Jacques's pronouncement, so he took the question at face value as a sign of the older man's confidence in him and appreciation for Mason visiting him. Mason smiled slightly and continued to feel his assurance growing. He decided not to waste any time with further pleasantries but merely began to launch into his prepared speech. He had been practicing it in front of the mirror in his tiny bathroom at home until he had it down pat and his words didn't stumble over each other, and now he was eager to unburden his concerns onto someone else with a longer history of experience with Dom Roberts and with Frédéric Averi.

"Jacques, I'm not here for a book. I need your advice."

"But of course. I am happy to advise you in any way I can.

I am not so busy now—as you can see for yourself. You are the first one to enter my shop today. Unfortunately, books in their physical form are not so often cherished these days, so my more faithful customers tend not to come in every moment. We are unlikely to be disturbed. So tell me how may I help you, my friend? You may speak freely."

"As you many remember, M. Averi has always hoped to expand and modernize the museum."

"Of course. That was always his dream, which we all hoped to eventually realize. Unfortunately, the dream never became a reality during my tenure there. Is it now finally going to happen? What do you say? That would make me very happy."

"It appears so. In preparation, I was charged with cataloguing the collection. I had been mainly working on the artwork and furnishings on view to the public. But then I thought about the items in storage …"

"Did Dom Roberts wish you to catalogue for him those as well?"

"He hadn't mentioned them specifically, but he's always so busy that I thought it slipped his mind or maybe I hadn't understood his directions carefully."

"And you were also uncomfortable reviewing your work-plan with him, so you merely guessed his intent. Is that it? Tell me."

"Exactly. Anyway, when I started looking at the figures for the items in storage, I found some things that didn't make any sense."

"In what way?"

"A few of the pieces that were sold to buyers seemed to have been valued too low, while others were insured too high."

"Are you sure of your calculations? What about the rest

of the collection—those in the public areas? Did you also find discrepancies to make you concerned about those items?"

"Those seem okay, which only makes me more suspicious."

"Suspicious?"

"Well, yes. You see, if my figures are off in general, then why does part of the collection's valuations make sense, and the other part's valuations don't?"

"Ah, I see what you mean."

"You do?"

"Of course. You think something is amiss. You are afraid the figures have been *fudged* as the Americans like to say … perhaps to allow greater insurance payments for items lost, or even, perhaps, they might mask loss of some funds for those items sold. Am I not correct? You see, I watch the crime stories as much as anyone else."

Mason wasn't quite sure if Jacques was still taking him seriously, but he decided to continue to take the older man at face value and forge ahead. "Yes. You're following my thinking exactly."

"Did you talk to Dom Roberts about your concerns yet?"

"No. I wanted to run them by you first."

"Ah. I see. And you trust me?"

"Of course. I know what the museum has meant to you and how long you worked there."

"Good. So let's see what must be done. Do you have copies of your files with you?" The older man pointed to Mason's trusty backpack, which the younger man still clutched nervously in his right hand and which he now gratefully relinquished to the other man by placing it on top of the counter of the bookshop. "Leave this with me and relax. As soon as I close the shop, I will start reviewing your work. I will be like your professor going over your homework for le Bac." He smiled at Mason as he took hold of the young man's treasured records.

"Do you think I should let Dom Roberts know that I consulted you?" Mason asked, beginning to feel some trepidation about going outside the expected chain of command at the museum. He couldn't bear to think of how he would deal with the possibility of the loss of his job if he ran afoul of his superior by having consulted with Jacques Charles. His job was what kept Mason grounded. It was what filled out most of his days. What would he possibly do if he lost it?

"Why don't you wait until I independently see what I make of the numbers before we decide that it is a gigantic financial scandal to be upset about? If you are correct, we can both go to him, and it will give our findings greater credence if we are both in agreement. Does that make sense to you?"

"Yes, it does," Mason said, relieved that any encounter with his superior was being temporarily delayed. At least he wouldn't have to think about it until he heard from Jacques; his mind could rest until then.

"Now get some fresh air. Take some deep breaths, and don't worry. Give me some time. I won't need so much, and I'll let you know as soon as I'm sure of what needs to be done." Jacques took Mason by the arm and led him out of the shop to enjoy the remains of the day, with the younger man now content in the knowledge that somehow everything would be all right.

5

A Picture in Silhouette

Mason couldn't believe how light his spirits felt. He had unburdened his worries onto his new partner in investigation and onto one in whom he had more confidence than in himself. It was as though he had a new lease on life. All the insecurities and worries of the past few weeks seemed to evaporate in the fresh air, which he breathed in after he left Jacques's shop. Mason decided to take the old man's advice and wandered over to the Jardin du Luxembourg as the best place where he could do so. It had been a long time since he had allowed himself the luxury of meandering through the gardens during the workday. In fact, he was sure he hadn't spent a whole afternoon there since his university days.

He entered the large wrought iron gates of the gardens and made his way over to the massive octagonal pond in front of the palais. He stood by one of the sides of the pond and took in the many colors of the assorted flowers surrounding it. The colors hit him head-on, and their brilliance seemed to reflect the new sense of optimism in his heart. Bright orange marigolds sparked in the sun, their tight heads forming a citrus blanket in front of the taller crimson poppies behind them. The gravel paths radiating out in different directions from the pond only occasionally blew sprays of their fine brown sand into his face because the day was still mild and the breezes subtle. Even the palm trees, tall and upright in green wooden planters set up around the periphery of the terrain, barely swayed in their sturdy boxes as the breezes blew.

He didn't want to sit down on the green benches or lie down on the patches of green grass designated for sunbathers also sharing the fair weather. Despite his lightness of heart, he still felt as though he had to be mobile. So he continued walking. He walked on past the playground, which was sheltered by tall, leafy trees. The light of the day still managed to cut through the leaves, dappling the ground in different patterns of light and shadow that played with his fancy.

He saw some children who were on swings and others who were climbing on jungle gyms. And he went closer to watch them play and share in their youthful enthusiasm. In one spot a metal cord had been extended on a slight incline between two tall poles. One by one, children rode down the incline in a rudimentary chair strapped to the cord. Each rider exhibited such glee in the descent that Mason had to stop there for a few minutes and watch their excitement in the motion of the slide. As each child finished the ride, he or she then methodically pushed the chair back up the cord for the next rider to take a turn. There was no chain of command here, just children enjoying each other's company.

It had been such a long time since he had felt free enough to engage in such delight, and for just one moment, he resolved to let all *l'art de vivre* of Paris become more of his way of life than it had previously been. He felt compelled to stay, watching each rider slide down the inclined metal cord and go back up, again and again—for how long he couldn't say. Then, as he continued watching the children's determined efforts to move each chair back up to the start of the ride, Mason suddenly realized that he had let his responsibilities go for too long. He felt a sense of guilt start to creep into him like a chill wind on a summer's day.

The light was now changing as the sun began to set. He had taken the afternoon off, but now he felt as though he needed to get back to work. His usual overwhelming sense of duty was re-lentlessly returning despite its brief and unaccustomed lapse. It was close to closing time for the museum, but that didn't worry him. He had his keys, and he often worked late after hours. In fact, that was the time when he did his most productive work— when the museum was mainly unoccupied and was as quiet and peaceful as a tomb. He would return there now.

Mason switched on the light to his office and sat down at his desk. The window behind him now provided no additional illumination to help him see better. The evening darkness had progressed to near blackness since he had left the Luxembourg gardens. As he turned on his computer, he saw the screensaver picture of his favorite painting in the museum coalesce before his eyes. It was the screensaver he had set up when he first started working at the museum. The picture seemed to get him motivated to do his best to protect the interests of the collection as he performed his daily analysis of its contents.

He adjusted his glasses to get the image into sharper focus; it was a particularly fine rendering by one of the lesser known Dutch Masters of a tavern scene, which was now installed on the upper floor of the museum. He loved the irreverence of the depiction of the bawdy figures, liberally imbibing wine, so unconcerned with their august positions, which were suggested by their sumptuous clothes and obvious wealth. The abandon of the portrayed figures was so distinct from his own restrained manner that he often delayed turning on his computer until he was sure no one was watching; he never wanted to be teased by the contrast between the picture and the image that most of his coworkers had of him. Only Odette, his new intern who also confessed to appreciating the picture, shared in his little secret, and in front of her he didn't need to guiltily shut down the machine to be sure no one was looking.

But now he was alone in the museum, and so he allowed himself a few moments to enjoy the picture on his computer console before plunging into his work. He cupped his chin in his hand and studied the facsimile of the original's elegant lines and then, with a sigh of resignation, began to finally delve into his many charts and numbers. Over the next hour, he continued his usual regimen and poured over the other figures that made so much more sense than those perplexing ones he had left with Jacques to help him decipher. He wondered if the older man had left his bookshop already and, after what he expected was a good meal for the evening, was at that very moment reviewing them.

Mason was still thinking about how soon he would know Jacques's results when he realized how tired he felt. All the worry of the recent days, the excursion to see Jacques, and the long walk through the gardens were finally demanding of him the need to rest. He knew he had finished enough work for the evening. He recalled the spasm of guilt he had felt earlier in the day for having left so much work unfinished, and he now felt his virtue renewed by making up for his unusual lapse; he felt that he should be rewarded. So he decided to treat himself to a viewing of his favorite portrait in its original form rather than its virtual representation before he went home to his small apartment and his late dinner alone. The painting was in its place of prominence in one of the rooms past the upstairs min-strels' gallery of the museum, and he would spend some time with it before he left the museum.

He lost sight of the pale copy of the painting as he turned off his computer and the machine shut down. He got up from his desk and turned off the office light so that he wouldn't have to come back to turn it off later. Mason walked back through the public rooms and up the central staircase, passing through the minstrels' gallery. For a moment, he thought he heard the sound of soft footsteps behind him, and he wondered whether one or another of the museum's security guards was still there and was making a spot check of the premises, which was done from time to time. He was thinking that if he were confronted, he would have to provide an explanation for why he was in this part of the museum and how he could avoid having anyone guess which painting he was dying to see. He wasn't in the mood to be teased.

But he never made it to see his favorite picture. As he ran the fingers of his left hand over the finely carved wood of the bal-ustrade, with a sickening feeling in his heart he felt the railing surprisingly give way. At the same time, he had the horrifying sensation of another's firm hand pushing violently against his back, even before he realized he was crashing through the rail-ing and falling over its delicate edge. Curiously, as he plunged closer and closer to the marble floor below, the disappointed feeling of loss flashed through his brain that he hadn't at least been able to take a last look at that painting he loved. He would also never know that, in some weird twist of fate, the outline of his body, as it finally hit the floor, would adopt a position as distorted as any one of those painted figures cavorting together in a tavern.

6

The Inspector Is Back on Duty

Aleixo Santos had been a security guard at Musée Averi for just two years. He had recently come to the depressing conclusion that working at the museum had not turned out to be as exciting as he thought it would be when he first started his employment. He was now living far from the nurturing warmth of his native Portugal, but Aleixo could still remember his father's parting words of encouragement when he left home determined to land a good employment position in Paris. His father had told him, "Keep far from the shady zones of others' affairs."

But instead of following his father's advice, Aleixo had settled on a career in security once in his new home, naively believing it would be a thrilling one. Aleixo had also hoped that Paris would be a city that would offer him more diverse adventures than those he had had in the small Portuguese town he had grown up in. But so far, both the city and the job had proved disappointing. And this morning he was feeling the sting of shattered dreams particularly acutely.

Aleixo had picked up his morning coffee earlier that day at his favorite *marché* to take with him while he made his usual rounds before the museum opened its doors to the public. He knew it was against the museum's rules to carry the steaming cup in his hands while he did so, but he was still in a slightly disgruntled mood and figured, as it was so early in the day, no one was to be the wiser for him flouting regulations. The coffee cup was still hot in his hand as he set it down on the bench by his locker to get dressed for his morning rounds. He quickly changed into his uniform, still preoccupied by his sense of disillusionment, and then started to leave the changing room only to realize with an annoyed start that the cup was still inside by his locker, cooling on the bench.

"*Droga*," he cursed softly in Portuguese, berating himself for his distraction. He turned to go back into the room to retrieve the cup when he saw the young, pretty intern, Odette, was also already in the museum. He liked her seriousness and the dedication she applied to her summer internship projects; it reminded him of his younger sister back at home whom he missed talking to. And, for a moment, his bad mood softened as he wondered whether he would be able to convince his father to let his sister join him in Paris. Perhaps she could share his apartment with him and help him with some of the housekeeping chores. Maybe she would also make him his morning cup of coffee before he left for work.

The intern, Odette, was always one of the first to arrive, and she was even liked by Aleixo's coworker Louis, who usually wasn't so accommodating as Aleixo was about allowing interns early entry to the museum, even one minute before public opening times.

"Bonjour, Odette. You're here early, as usual." He greeted her in French, proud that his grasp of his second language was now almost as good as his native Portuguese.

"Bonjour, Aleixo. Yes. Louis scolded me but let me in after some coercion. I wanted to help Mason by checking the dimensions of a few of the pieces in the gallery upstairs. That is my assignment for the day, and I wanted to get a head start on it."

"That sounds like information he should already know for himself," Aleixo grumbled, once more annoyed when he thought about how Mason had got to spend so much time in close proximity with such a sweet, young girl. Knowing that foolish Mason, he hadn't even appreciated it, Aleixo thought to himself.

"He says it's good for me to be able to visually estimate the numbers, but I think he really wants me to learn to appreciate the pieces themselves that he loves the best. He says I have a tendency to value them by size instead of *masterfulness*." Odette laughed softly.

Aleixo could tell that the reproof the girl had received from Mason in the course of her internship had actually stung her teenage pride a bit—and more so than she was letting on. He decided to encourage her to stand up more for herself as he would his sister. He felt she just needed a push in the right direction. "Well, don't let anyone boss you around too much."

"I won't," Odette answered as she headed toward the public area and on to the gallery.

After she left, Aleixo realized, once again, that he still hadn't picked up his coffee, which was now probably ice cold. He made up his mind that nothing else would deter him from catching those tasty, bitter sips, which were the best part of his morning routine. But even before he could put his hand on the knob to open the door to the changing room, he was stopped in his tracks by the sound of Odette's piercing screams. They came from the central area of the museum and echoed against the marble floors and walls of the museum, reverberating again and again as he dashed toward the origin of the sound.

Raynaud sat next to his anguished daughter, his strong, muscular arm encircling her slender shoulders as Odette continued to sob uncontrollably. He was, at least, reassured that the erratic sounds coming from her trembling lips now had less of a hysterical inflection to them than they had when he had first arrived at the museum.

Odette had called his cell phone, and she had been so distraught that he had struggled to decipher what she was attempting to communicate. His initial thought had been that she was somehow injured, and in a rare occurrence for his usual state of unruffled calm, he had felt his heart beat in his chest with more vigor than he was used to. The thought had also run through his mind that if anything had happened to her, how would he relay the news to his ex-wife, Josephine? That thought had caused him added angst. After all, he had been entrusted with Odette's safety and security for the summer; it was his sole responsibility, and no one else's, to make sure his time with her was unmarred by any calamity of any kind. He knew that if anything went wrong, even of a minor nature, it would be the last time he would be allowed this luxury of extended father-daughter engagement together.

The two museum security guards—he had been informed by Odette, who had managed to tell him this through her sobs, that their names were Aleixo and Louis—stood grimly in front of them. Odette had also told her father that upon hearing her screams, both men had run from opposite directions of the museum to the source of the screams to find her overcome with horror as she pointed a small, shaking finger at the prostrate figure of Mason Henri. The young man had been lying in a heap on the floor below the upper gallery from which he had obviously plunged, and even to her unpracticed eyes, it was clear he was not moving and no longer alive.

Now the body had been removed from its grotesque position, but in between her now-fractured sobs, Raynaud knew
that Odette was still trying her best to describe to him what she
had first come upon; this was despite his valiant attempts to get
the frightening image out of her mental consciousness, at least
until she was better able to handle it.

There were also two *agents de police* from the *Préfecture de
Police de Paris* who had arrived first; they had poured over the
area, which was now cordoned off from the rest of the museum.
Now they stood silently together, their heads nodding in unison
as they listened carefully to the two male detectives who had
just arrived from the *Police Judiciaire*, the criminal investigation
department. The latter two had come to also look over the site
and obviously take charge of it.

Raynaud sized up the detectives as best he could even as
he continued to comfort Odette. The older one appeared to
be in his midfifties. He was accompanied by a younger man,
likely in his thirties. Their relative rank was easily discernible to
Raynaud by the respectful deference the younger man gave to
the other. Raynaud had significant experience with partnership
arrangements, and he could discern by the younger man's close
attention to the occasional hand gestures of his partner that the
older detective was worthy of some respect; he was methodically examining the outline on the floor, which was all that was
left to prove that Mason's crumpled body had ever been there.

"Inspector, may I speak with you?" Raynaud asked in
French, getting up and leaving Odette for the first time since
he had arrived. His own analytic instincts had risen up to the
surface in the face of the other detectives' interaction with each
other; he went over to the two but had really addressed his
question solely to the senior man. That burly investigator, who
had the appearance of one used to such scenarios as the one he'd

come upon that morning, looked up from the crime scene at Raynaud. But Raynaud knew that the French detective had also been surreptitiously sizing him up from the corner of his eye, although only one knowledgeable in the practiced technique would have ever guessed it.

"Yes?" the French detective asked brusquely.

"I would like to introduce myself. I'm Inspector Alain Raynaud. I'm Canadian, with the Service de Police de la Ville de Montréal. I have been visiting my daughter, Odette, in Paris for the summer. She has been interning here in the museum, and she called me to be with her considering what has occurred." Raynaud looked back over his shoulder at his daughter who still appeared tremulous, and he gave her an encouraging smile before turning back to the other man.

"I will then also introduce myself. I am Inspector Georges Lanier from the Police Judiciaire. As I understand it, your daughter found M. Henri, correct?" His accent suggested to Raynaud that his native tongue might be more at home in the northwestern limits of France, perhaps Brittany.

"Yes, and then the museum security guards arrived after her."

"Did your daughter know M. Henri well?"

"She was helping him this summer. He was cataloguing the museum's collection."

"Yes, that is what information the two agents have already obtained and provided to me. Let me ask you. Did your daughter observe any strange or despondent behavior on the part of M. Henri to suggest that he would have taken his own life in such a dramatic manner as this?"

"None whatsoever from what my daughter has told me," Raynaud answered, choosing to ignore the touch of sarcasm obvious in the other detective's inflection.

"I see. Well, such feelings aren't always apparent to some-one else, especially to one so young." Now Inspector Lanier himself looked back at Odette, as if a second look were neces-sary to confirm his initial impression of her. He then turned back to Raynaud. "But rest assured, we will be looking at all possibilities. It was quite a drop from that height." Now Lanier raised his eyes, dark brown under black, bushy eyebrows with flecks of gray in them, matching in color the thick head of hair on his rather large head; he was scanning with those eyes up from the marble floor to the broken railing of the gallery above.

All at once, the sharp tapping sounds of shoes quickly pounding against the floor could be heard reverberating from the other side of the room. Both men instinctively followed the sound to see a man appear. He was dressed in a navy-blue suit, a crisp white shirt, and a deep crimson and navy paisley cravat around his neck, which seemed even more out of place than it otherwise would have considering the scene about him. His hair had been closely cropped, obscuring the line between his bald head and his remaining hair.

Before any of the detectives could speak, the new arrival offered an introduction. "I'm Dom Roberts. I was informed of this great tragedy, and I came over as soon as I could get here."

He moved over to the group of men with an alacrity that was consistent with his trim physique. He rapidly insinuated himself into the circle formed by Raynaud, Lanier, and Lanier's partner, who was now introduced as Inspector Jules Pecor.

Lanier addressed the new arrival. "M. Roberts, you help manage the museum for M. Frédéric Averi, I believe? That is what I have been told."

"That is quite correct. I'm devastated by what has occurred here today. Totally devastated. It's quite unbelievable."

"It appears that the fall was more likely to have occurred

last night, to be exact. We will, of course, be able to get an exact time of death going forward."

"Yes, of course," Roberts agreed. "You correct me, Inspector."

"Was M. Henri often in the habit of working late by himself?"

"Yes, I believe he was."

"And would you have any reason to believe someone might have harbored any ill will toward M. Henri?"

"Just what are you suggesting?" Roberts asked, the pitch of his voice rising slightly higher as his body seemed to extend up above his medium height; he leaned closer toward Lanier as though he hadn't heard him correctly.

"I am not suggesting anything." Lanier continued, apparently unperturbed by Roberts's show of disbelief. Lanier's monotone speaking voice remained totally unchanged. "I am merely attempting to understand the situation I now find myself needing to analyze. That is all."

"Oh. Then in answer to your question: No. I can only think that Mason allowed the stress and strain of his employment to get the better of him. He was a very diligent worker. I am horrified to think how this unhappy event will affect M. Averi and his beloved museum—totally horrified. Quite unbelievable."

"You haven't been in contact yet with M. Averi?"

"No. I wanted to assess the situation for myself first before speaking with him. M. Averi is a very busy man."

"Yes. That is a very reasonable way to proceed. But even one so busy as M. Averi will be sure to need to make time for an event such as this."

During the interchange, Raynaud stood silent as a statue, taking the time to observe each man as they interacted. It was apparent to him that the two, who had such different mannerisms, had taken an instant dislike toward each other, although Roberts seemed to have been mollified by the inspector's last statement agreeing with his initial decision.

"I think I have enough for now, and we should return to the Police Judiciaire. What do you say, Pecor?" Without waiting for his junior partner's acquiescence, Lanier then said, "M. Roberts, I suggest you now contact M. Averi. We will allow you to do that at this time." He dismissed Roberts and turned back to Raynaud, motioning for them to move closer to Odette.

As Raynaud and Lanier stood together, Lanier said quietly, "I suggest that you now remove your daughter from this environment. It cannot be good for her. I would, as one inspector to another, also hint that my hands may be, not necessarily tied, but let us say *hampered* in some slight way by M. Averi's and, by extension, M. Robert's connections ... if I am reading my signs correctly. But should you have any thoughts on this matter that come to mind, feel free to contact me. I will make time for you. Here. I will give you my card; it has a number on it where I may be reached."

Lanier then looked at Pecor and jerked his head to the side. Pecor obviously understood the sign, and the two men walked together toward the museum's exit.

"Odette, I think I should take you home now," Raynaud said to his daughter, taking her by the arm and raising her up from her seat. Shielding her vision as best he could from the drawn outline of where Mason's body had been, which was still clearly marked out on the floor, Raynaud guided Odette from the museum by the same route the two French detectives had taken as he silently contemplated Lanier's last few words to him.

When Raynaud arrived home with Odette, he immediately asked her the question that had been nagging at him ever since he got to the museum and saw for himself what had occurred. It was only his concern for his daughter that had caused him to delay speaking with her about it until they were back in the apartment they were sharing for the summer and Odette appeared to be returning somewhat to her usual self.

"Odette, what exactly was Mason cataloguing? Be specific."

"Just the museum's collection, like I told you before," Odette said.

She then looked down at her hands, and Raynaud knew there was something else that she was debating whether to bring up. He sensed that she was weighing her loyalties between her father and her recent friend, Mason, who was no longer able to defend himself. He also knew he had to refrain from his usual brusque manner of probing further and further into an issue. Despite their established geographical distance from each other, there was still an extremely strong bond between them, so Raynaud sensed that if he waited patiently for his daughter to continue speaking, she would soon do so. And it would be better if she came to what she wanted to tell him at her own speed. He was not disappointed.

"He might have found something I didn't mention to the agents."

"What was it?" he asked.

"Mason told me he had found some discrepancies in the valuations of some of the items he hadn't really been charged to look at on his own," Odette began. "He wasn't sure about them, though, and decided to run them by an older man named Jacques Charles—someone he said he felt he could trust. Mason said Monsieur Charles used to have Mason's position at the museum."

"Do you know if Mason ever spoke to Jacques Charles?"

"No, but I think he was going to."

"All right. Don't mention this to anyone else just yet. Let me see what I can find out. At the right time, I'll take it further to Lanier. Anyway, that's enough of this for one day. I think you've had more than enough excitement to last you through the summer."

"Papa, you promise you won't let them imply anything bad about Mason?" She looked pleadingly into her father's eyes.

"I promise," Raynaud answered more confidently than he felt.

7

Two Take the Lead

Jessica, on the lookout for Alain, scanned the teeming throngs of tourists circling the Panthéon, the grand eighteenth-century structure containing the tombs of many of France's most famous citizens. Alain had asked her to meet him there, as it was most likely she would be able to easily find such a prominent Parisian landmark even as such a new arrival to Paris. He had filled her in on all that he knew about Mason's untimely death, which he had learned from what he had observed at Musée Averi and what he had managed to obtain from Odette's description of events. He had suggested the next best move was that they speak directly to Jacques Charles, who had his book business nearby and who Alain felt was the most likely person to shed some light on what Mason might have uncovered prior to his untimely death.

As Jessica stood in front of the massive edifice, waiting once again for her reliable partner in investigation, she thought back to Tom's initial request for her help. She had been tasked to learn what she could about Frédéric Averi's global operations, and if there were any irregularities, had they contributed to Lucy's unhappiness due to her reliance on one of Averi's business concerns? Jessica had agreed to help more as a need to satisfy an old friend than for any great confidence in her ability to succeed at the job entrusted to her; she was unsure if there was anything questionable at all about Averi's business practices and, if there was, that she would be able to parse it out. But now there was a young man dead. And although it might be unrelated to what she was originally asked to look into, if there was something nefarious going on, she couldn't help but wonder about fate. It had led her once again to be an unlikely investigator of such a serious situation.

She also wondered if there was some unconscious quirk of Alain's that had led him to suggest this very meeting place to get together before they both confronted Monsieur Jacques Charles. She knew that Jacques Charles's bookshop was close by, but she couldn't fail to note the irony of Alain's choice of the meeting place: a monument to the dead. She turned away from the crowds for a moment to gaze up at the neoclassical building; its portico, adorned with Corinthian columns and a triangular pediment stationed in front of the huge dome rising up to the sky, seemed a suitably sober cover for the crypts entombed below. Maybe Alain's choice was an appropriate one after all.

Scolding herself for being somewhat morbid, Jessica decided to redirect her attention to the many living people around her, and as though granted a desired reward, she finally saw Alain coming out of the crowd toward her. After they had moved away to a rare unoccupied corner of the large plaza, they were able to speak to each other far from the din of the crowd.

She asked, "So how's Odette doing? I was so worried about her when you told me what happened. And poor Mason. He had seemed such a decent sort."

"She'll survive. But obviously it wasn't a very pleasant sight that she had to witness, to say the least. She's likely to be feeling the effects of it all for a while. That's one thing I'm discouraged by."

"Alain ..."

"Yes, Jessica? What is it?"

"I'm worried that I pressured you into involving Odette in something that she didn't have any need to get involved in, especially at her impressionable age. It's been bothering me so much ever since I heard the news about Mason."

"Nonsense. Whatever Mason came across—if he did come across anything worth pursuing—he would have done so whether or not we arrived at the museum to take a look around for ourselves. If just scouting out one of Averi's holdings led to Mason's death, we have more power and influence than I would have thought possible. Mason may have taken his own life, or he may have been helped along the way. At this point, we just don't know which is correct. But from what Lanier implied, the need by those in power to keep Averi's name away from any scandal may make it one hard nut to crack to get to the truth of the matter ... if the truth causes embarrassment, or worse, for the powerful. But, Jessica, stop worrying about it, and let's go over now to Jacques Charles's bookshop and see what we can find out there as a start. That's all we can do at the present."

They walked away from the Panthéon's large plaza, and after leaving the density of people behind them, they soon spotted the tiny shop they were looking for. It was one of the old-fashioned varieties of typically French storefronts. It had varnished wooden siding supporting large glass windows on either side of the entrance. In the windows, books of many sizes with aging bindings were arranged in such a way as to best catch the eye of anyone who might happen to pass by. Jessica thought the shop looked like it might have seen better days in its time.

Alain pushed open the door of the shop, and as the overhead bells rang out at the entrance, they saw an older man come over to greet them from the back of the store.

"Bonjour," he said.

"For my companion's benefit, may we converse together in English?" Alain immediately requested, smiling slightly at Jessica as he spoke.

She gave a sigh of relief. She had no illusions about her level of comprehension of the French language and had no wish to have to wait until after the interview to receive a paraphrased report from Alain as to what had transpired.

"But of course. What may I do for you?" the shopkeeper politely responded in English.

"May we presume you are Monsieur Jacques Charles himself?"

"Yes. You may. And may I ask now in what way I may be of assistance to you both?" he repeated, looking appraisingly at Alain and Jessica.

"Monsieur Charles, were you acquainted with Monsieur Mason Henri?" Raynaud asked abruptly.

"Why yes, but why do you say it like that? Why *were*? Has something happened to him?" The shopkeeper now looked even more closely at the two newcomers to his store, as though to seek an answer to his question merely from a study of their faces.

Jessica found herself struggling not to let her usual sense of ferment at these times reveal itself on her own face.

"I am sorry to inform you that M. Henri is now deceased. I must admit I am a little surprised you haven't heard the news," Alain continued. "I would have thought you would have."

"But why? No. That cannot be. He was so young."

"We assure you it is a fact. Have you been in contact with him recently?"

"Monsieur, excuse me, but I must first ask who you are and how you know about this sad occurrence and why you both come to see me about it. It is very unusual."

"Your question is understandable." Raynaud turned to Jessica and said, "This is Dr. Jessica Shepard, and I am Inspector Alain Raynaud. We are here in no official capacity. I wouldn't want to mislead you as to that. We are not with French police. In fact, I am Canadian, and Dr. Shepard, American, but we were briefly acquainted with Mason Henri. In fact, my daughter was even better acquainted with him, as she had been working under his tutelage at Musée Averi. Are you aware that he was found to have fallen at Musée Averi, and he succumbed to his injuries?"

"No. I wasn't aware of that," M. Charles said thoughtfully.

"We have had information that he might have wanted to speak to you about some concerns he had. We wondered whether he met with you or at least spoke with you?"

"I am not sure I should be discussing this with the two of you, but yes, as a matter of fact, he did come to see me—and quite recently. He was worried about some figures he was reviewing for the museum. You see, previously—before I ran this shop—I used to be employed by the museum in a somewhat similar capacity to Mason's, and he wanted my opinion as to what I thought. That is all."

"And did you determine that he was right to be *worried*?"

"Since I did not, I don't feel I am doing anything wrong in talking to you about this. He had left me copies of some of his findings, but I saw that there was nothing much there. When I couldn't reach him after I reviewed what he left me, I assumed either he had decided to take a short vacation—it's a good time of year for that, you would agree—or he had decided to show them to his superiors at the museum, and they told him what I would have. I would even show you some of what he left with me, but I tossed the copies when I realized there was nothing there for him to fret about. I figured I could reassure him when I next saw him by chance or when I finally heard back from him."

"That is unfortunate. Can you give us some idea of what specifically he had asked your advice about?"

"Why yes. You see, he thought some valuations were not correct, and I guess he worried that they weren't off due to mere carelessness. But he made some miscalculations—that is not infrequently the case—and I didn't find anything he should have been uneasy about. You see, he wasn't employed there for so long. Sometimes there is a need to prove oneself useful when one is relatively new at a job, and it can blind the eye that experience improves the vision of."

Jessica looked as though she would like to ask more questions, but Alain laid his hand on her arm, signaling he was convinced that they would gain no further insights and only risk antagonizing someone they might need to consult again in the future. She accepted the slight pressure of his hand as her restraint and allowed him to merely say without interruption, "Thank you, M. Charles. We appreciate the time you have given us."

"Not at all. Not at all. I am only so saddened by the news you have brought me," he replied. "It was a terrible shock to me. I am not sure how I will get over it."

Jessica opened the door of her apartment to find Madame Clair standing proudly, or as proudly as her diminutive frame would allow. Behind the concierge were Alain and Odette, making up the rear guard. They were both overburdened with enormous shopping bags, which had obviously been filled at a spectacular food shop specializing in all sorts of culinary delicacies if the pungent aroma that attacked Jessica's nose was any clue; the smells emanating from the packages were delightful, although a bit overpowering for the relatively close confines of the enclosed hallway outside Jessica's door. Madame Clair pushed past Jessica with a level of authority more suggestive of a field marshal. She headed toward the kitchen in the back of the hall with every appearance of someone possessed of intimate knowledge of the inner workings of Jessica's rental apartment, which was only one of her dominion.

After leaving Jacques Charles's bookshop on the Left Bank, Jessica and Alain had decided that it was the best course of action to take a short break from their inquiry and plan the next steps of attack. They also felt that a brief spell of normalcy was needed and would be a good thing for Odette to engage in after the recent shock she had received at the museum. So Alain had offered to create a dinner for the three of them primarily consisting of Odette's favorite dish: *soupe de poisson*. And he and Odette had offered to do all the shopping if Jessica provided the location for the feast.

Madame Clair returned from the kitchen and said, "I have opened the cabinets and found a large enough pot for you to use, M. Raynaud." She strained her neck to look directly up at him with her additional instructions. "It is good and heavy and will help you make a soup that is *merveilleuse*." She snapped her fingers to emphasize her point. "Now, I will leave you all to do the cooking." She laughed and shut the door firmly behind her after giving Jessica, Alain, and Odette a satisfied cluck of her tongue as her final parting gift.

"Well, she certainly knows more about my borrowed kitchen than I do," Jessica said disconsolately. "I'm sure she'll be telling everyone else in the building who will listen what a sorry case I am. It was probably obvious to her I hadn't opened those cabinets once except to search for a coffee mug. I don't even have a clue as to what's in there."

"Don't worry. Papa is really a good cook … and I am even better," Odette added, laughing at her own joke.

"Come on. Stop bragging, and let's make some soup!" Alain demanded.

The bags were unloaded onto the counters of the tiny kitchen. Jessica watched in awe and wondered how such a diverse array of ingredients were possibly needed for a mere soup; each item was laid out with almost scientific precision by father and daughter in an exhaustive *mise en place*. The essential ingredient, the red mullet fish, came out of the bags first, followed by a huge bottle of olive oil, bright red tomatoes, garlic, savory onions, leeks, fennel, and then small jars of individually labeled spices: cayenne pepper, saffron, salt, and black pepper. Last, out come a large bag of crumbly croutons and cheese for shredding, the latter of which was so fragrant that Jessica was afraid the small kitchen would be engulfed by the smell for weeks on end.

It ran through Jessica's mind that after this meal she would definitely have to follow up with Madame Clair about where the cleaning items were stored. This was not going to be an easy job to clean up after. But this was Paris, so she let a sense of culinary enthusiasm flow through her veins.

The three working together in cooperative effort soon had heated the fish and vegetables in the hot oil, strained and milled the solid ingredients, and recombined them with the others so that, in seemingly no time, a delicious creation was ready in front of them for enjoyment. The pièce de résistance was a bowl of toasts, slathered with garlicky rouille and the cheese that was now grated and ready to thicken the fragrant steaming concoction.

After the meal, Jessica and Alain left Odette in the living room to call a close friend of hers to chat like any healthy teenager would want to after having shared her dinner with two adults. They began the arduous task of at least superficially cleaning up after the cooking session they had indulged in so enthusiastically.

Alone in the kitchen, Jessica said, "Alain, we didn't learn that much from Charles, did we? All he basically implied was that Mason wasn't on to anything improper—if we can believe him, that is. What do you think about him? What's your take?"

"I'm not sure yet. He was hard to evaluate. He may be all that he appears to be—or he may not. I think it's still too early to tell. What I'm sure of at this point, though, is that we need to get in to see Frédéric Averi himself. That's the only way we'll learn more that's of any use."

"Do you think that will be very hard to do?" Jessica asked.

"Not necessarily. We've met Dom Roberts already, at least briefly. It's possible we can use that to get to see Averi."

"I agree. I think that makes a lot of sense."

"Why, thank you."

"You're very welcome. Anyway, when do you think we should try?"

"Odette's talking to her friend Marie now. I'm going to suggest she spend some time with Marie and her family because I don't want Odette any further involved in this for a while. Odette doesn't want to go back to the museum yet; she's just not ready, and she told me the same was suggested to her by the museum. Once I have her squared away, I think you and I need to see Dom Roberts again and Frédéric Averi. I've already checked on the location of Averi's corporate headquarters here in Paris. That's the most sensible place to get in to see him. We'll start there and see what we come up with."

"Good. I'm all in on the plan. I think it makes a lot of sense."

"Fine. So let's tackle these dishes," Alain noted. "Believe me, next time I'll suggest an easy American dish like hamburgers!"

"Ha ha ha," Jessica said, smacking Alain on the back with her well-used dish towel.

8

The Ride Begins

The headquarters of Averi Industries was located in La Défense, the modern business district three kilometers west of the city limits of Paris. It was a stretch of tall glass and steel buildings forming a distinct metamorphosis from the more classical skyline of central Paris that Jessica had begun to feel almost familiar with. The headquarters was not far from the striking boxlike structure of La Grande Arche, which served as a kind of totem for the area.

Jessica and Alain had arranged a meeting with Frédéric Averi through his subordinate, Dom Roberts. It had been surprisingly easy. Alain had predicted correctly that his brief interaction with Roberts at Musée Averi had provided the means for allowing them to put a foot in the door of the corporation's portals. Alain hadn't needed to, or had not thought it advisable as of yet, to mention his prior experience assessing security at some of the larger art museums in Paris; he had kept that personal information in his breast pocket if needed later.

As they entered the building housing Averi Industries, Jessica was able to observe firsthand the diversity of its corporate holdings: a large brass plaque over the marble reception desk listed the numerous subsidiaries scattered across the globe.

The receptionist was supported in her labors by two huge security guards, one on either side of her, whose uniforms bore the same company insignia that Jessica recognized from those she had previously seen at Averi's museum. But these guards bore no resemblance to the kinder, gentler Aleixo and Louis described by Alain as having helped and comforted Odette after her discovery of Mason's body. These two looked like they wouldn't accept any breach of the corporate policy handed down to them from above. She was glad Alain had the foresight to arrange a formal appointment, confident that if they had just shown up unannounced, they would have been politely but summarily escorted off the premises.

Instead, Jessica and Alain were escorted up to the top floor of the building where Dom Roberts soon greeted them personally. The penthouse area was very large. It seemed to stretch for miles, unencumbered by any furnishings of any kind, to a broad bank of floor-to-ceiling windows that provided a bird's-eye view to the many other corporate complexes in the neighborhood below.

Roberts stood with his back toward the windows so that Jessica got her first glance of Frédéric Averi's associate unimpaired by any cast of shadows that might have obscured him. Roberts was slim and trim—those were the words that flashed through her mind at a first glance of appraisal. But she didn't have much time to formulate any other descriptive adjectives because the gentleman in question immediately began speaking to them at breakneck speed.

"Of course, we will converse in English for Dr. Shepard's benefit. I believe you mentioned she was American. I remember you, Inspector Raynaud, but as I did not yet meet your attractive companion, I am happy to do so now. I would also like to take this opportunity to say that I understand how traumatic

Mademoiselle Odette's experience must have been for her. I hope she is now doing well. It has shaken us all, especially M. Averi—of that I can assure you. That is why such a busy man as M. Averi has consented to make time to meet you both today. It is not a common occurrence, to say the least."

As soon as Roberts finished speaking, the intricately carved wooden doors of the inner office slid open to either side. They did so as if on cue, and for a moment, Jessica wondered if Frédéric Averi might have been surreptitiously observing them from the moment they first arrived in the building. Roberts led Jessica and Alain through the open doors to meet the head of Averi Industries.

M. Averi was seated behind a large glass and chrome desk notable for the absence of any papers on it. The sole item on the desk was a computer console. It was positioned off to one side and obviously attested to the fact that a man such as M. Averi would have no need for papers; the digital world would be his oyster. The top of the desk was as shiny as a well-polished mirror without a speck of dust on it, and Jessica found it hard to direct her attention away from the reflected version of the man toward the flesh-and-blood one seated behind it. He was ensconced in a generous leather chair with a brown, tricolor cowhide pattern, which was just still visible at the edges behind Averi's large frame.

M. Averi appeared to be in his fifties. He had thick black hair with just the requisite graying at the temples. His appearance made Jessica think of an advertisement for great movers and shakers of the corporate world that she might have seen in a business magazine. But he was dressed casually in a white linen shirt with long sleeves kept in place by gold cufflinks. He wore no jacket and no tie. The massive gold watch on his left wrist was the only other obvious accoutrement that suggested his obvious financial success.

Jessica and Alain were escorted deeper into the sanctuary to two chairs positioned to the other side of M. Averi's desk; Jessica could see, without any surprise, that they seemed to be positioned slightly lower to the ground than that of M. Averi's. Averi rose graciously from his desk to greet them.

"Ah, here are the visitors I have been told to expect. How do you do?" He waited the requisite few moments before continuing. "I understand from Dom that you have some questions about the unfortunate event that recently occurred at my museum. It was a tragedy, to say the least. But I have been in consult with my legal advisors, and they have advised me that I may listen to your questions to determine if I may answer them. They did not feel they needed to be present at this time." He looked pointedly at Jessica and Alain before continuing to speak. "Unfortunately, I have just—only a few minutes ago—been summoned to my château in the Loire Valley because of some difficulties with the renovations that are ongoing there."

Although disappointed, Jessica said, "If this is an inconvenient time, we can return on another day. Perhaps tomorrow?" She was unwilling to allow them to be put off any later than that.

"You misunderstand me, young lady. Why there is no reason for you both to return after you have come here to see me. Nonsense. I was merely going to offer that you both accompany me to my château. We will be able to speak on our drive to the hangar where I keep my helicopter. It is on the outskirts of the city, so we will have some time to converse in the car on the way over there. Then, if you are both agreeable, I would like to invite you to continue by helicopter to complete the journey to Château Averi with me. I can tell you it is quite an adrenaline rush to see Paris from the air this way—even if we can't fly directly over it. And I am always eager to have new arrivals witness the transformations we are making at Château Averi. We have some monumental plans for it. Don't we, Dom?"

He looked at his assistant briefly but failed to wait for any response before precipitously turning back to Jessica and Alain and continuing to speak. "Rest assured, I will have the pilot return you to wherever you wish to go once we are done."

Jessica cast a furtive glance at Alain, with what she could only guess were pleading eyes. She realized this might be her only chance at such an unexpected adventure, simultaneously rationalizing that they would be avoiding any delay in talking with Averi if they didn't have to come back the next day. Also, she weighed the fact in her mind that the closeness of the setting in a private car and helicopter might induce greater openness on Averi's part, allowing them to learn things they otherwise might not be able to. She hoped, at least, that same thought was running through Alain's mind.

With agreement obtained from her companion in arms by the nod of his head, they descended to the extensive corporate garage maintained below the headquarters of Averi Industries. Jessica soon found herself sitting in a black stretch limousine between Alain to her left and M. Averi to her right. The limo left the garage to head to the helicopter hangar that housed Averi's means of transportation to his château. Jessica wondered how often this magnate of global industry popped back and forth this way between Paris and the Loire Valley. Roberts was in the front passenger seat, seated next to the liveried driver, whose black cap added a touch of formality to their travel arrangements.

"So what is it that you are both most interested in or concerned about?" Averi asked once the car was moving at a good steady clip toward the helicopter hangar. "You must know we at Averi Industries are all distraught about what happened. Musée Averi is one of my greatest passions, and it has hurt me to the core to see such a sad event occur there. It is very distressing. It is always a shocking affair when a faithful employee takes his own life, and especially so when it is done in such a theatrical manner as M. Henri chose to take."

"Are you so sure it was suicide?" Alain asked quietly.

"But what else could it be?" Averi asked incredulously. "I do not think he would have fallen by accident."

Dom Roberts chimed in, turning his head back over his left shoulder from the front seat to join the conversation. "It's not as though there was no railing. This is absurd."

"Don't mind Dom. He is very protective of the reputation of the museum, as I am, of course. It is very unfortunate that that particular area of the museum isn't yet under video surveillance, which would have allowed confirmation of the nature of the suicide. That is because it is primarily a gallery that leads toward the inner rooms where the more significant artwork is exhibited. But that omission will be rapidly corrected. Rest assured on that point."

"Yes. I was wondering about that very omission," Alain said before he pressed on. "I was considering, though, the question of whether he might have been pushed."

"Pushed, did you say?" Averi asked, with the first hint of sarcasm now evident in his deep voice. "I cannot believe I am hearing you correctly. Now really, we are not in a *roman policier.*"

Jessica saw Alain mentally weigh how much further to take the line of questioning he was putting to Averi before he finally said, "Perhaps Mason Henri came upon something that he shouldn't have? Eh?"

"I am not sure I approve of what questions he is asking you, M. Averi," Roberts said loudly, looking directly at his employer—or as directly as he could, considering that his position in the front passenger seat forced him to practically spin his neck around like an owl to speak to his boss.

"Dom, remain calm. Remain calm. I am sure our guests meant no obvious offense. I can't imagine they were seriously implying anything sinister would go on in my museum." Then Averi leaned across Jessica to get closer to Alain and said, "Again, rest assured, we will be looking into all projects M. Henri was involved in, but I am confident all is well, and it will turn out as I said—that he merely allowed himself to be overwhelmed by his dedication and unfortunately didn't seek the help he needed to deal with his troubles. Perhaps he was afraid of a stigma or discounted his own demons. Who can say what possessed him? After all, I am a businessman and not a psychiatrist. Now, I think that is all I am obligated to—or should—discuss with you both. And anyway, here we are at the hangar, right on time. Perfect timing as it actually is. Let me be your host, and let's see Paris from the sky. I have promised you a treat, and you shall have one; I think there will be an even greater one when we reach our final destination. And then I will be happy to give you a personal tour of my château. I believe it is magnificent, and perhaps Doctor Shepard—"

"Jessica, please," she interrupted.

"Jessica, of course. Perhaps, Jessica, you will especially appreciate the extensive gardens of my estate. They are truly magnificent this time of year. We will be sure to tour them as well as the château. Do not worry about that."

Averi, Roberts, Alain, and Jessica got out of the limousine at the hangar, and Jessica soon found herself strapped into her seat, with headset in place, in Averi's private helicopter. Her three companions and the pilot were similarly outfitted for the ride. As the helicopter climbed straight up into the sky and she soon saw Paris spread out beneath her gaze, the adrenaline rush that Averi had alerted her to expect overcame her. She could see familiar landmarks: the Eiffel Tower, the Seine, the Louvre. They appeared truly phenomenal from the bird's-eye view of the helicopter.

But then the view below began to homogenize as they left the city altogether. Greens and browns, the colors subtly blending into each other, transformed the undulating landscape below into a soft mélange of natural colors. The headset she wore cocooned her in her own little world, but the view itself engrossed her. She had no wish for further conversation as the helicopter traveled along in its path toward Averi's château.

After what seemed to be too short a time to experience all that she wanted to feel, Jessica caught site of an opening in the woodlands, and in the center of the patch of greenery was the huge château they were here to see. It was surrounded by a moat. Behind the château, the extensive gardens Averi had promised were laid out in formal arrangements. Even from the height of the helicopter, she could make out numerous large, green yew trees, which had been sculpted into striking conical forms of immense proportions; they rose up from the centers of boxwood enclosures. It flashed through her mind that she should have thought to bring along a large sun hat and a basket full of gardening gloves, clippers, and a trowel so that she could roam the gardens and perform her own horticultural artistry, if it would be allowed to a mere guest. Or, perhaps, she could just wander among the broad gravel paths that crisscrossed through the vast gardens and converged to meet by a huge fountain in the center, which was spouting sprays of water up into the air.

Before she could indulge any further in her daydreams, the

helicopter started to descend onto a generous courtyard in the back of the château. As the aircraft got closer and closer to the ground, it blew up huge clouds of gravel dust in front of it as the whirling blades above their heads unsettled the ground beneath them. The dust made it hard to visualize anything, and Jessica was brought back precipitously to earth, making a silent prayer that the pilot would be able to see well enough through the dust storm to safely land. But they landed without incident, and several minutes later all the passengers jumped down without injury from the helicopter to the courtyard.

"Welcome to Château Averi," the proud landowner said as he corralled them together around him for the beginning of the tour. "Let's go to the front so that you can see my home from the view that I think it is best appreciated."

Jessica and Alain followed Averi and Roberts past what appeared to be large stables. At one point, many years ago, they must have been the home of numerous horses, judging from the capacious size of the structure. Jessica thought it now more likely that the buildings housed a fleet of expensive cars to chauffer the owner and his guests to other grand mansions in the vicinity rather than the carriages previously stored there. The group made their way around the side of the buildings and came upon massive stone steps that led up to the front entrance of the château.

Jessica stood for a moment at the base of the steps and looked up. She needed to take in the view from her own angle of perspective as Averi had suggested. The picture was as magnificent as he had said it would be. Now she could better understand the pride he took in its ownership, which had resonated in his voice when they first arrived. The massive Baroque, pale-stone edifice rose up grandly from the staircase, and the black slates on its extensive roof glistened in the bright sunshine.

Floor-to-ceiling windows ran across its façade, topped with additional semicircular windows so that as much daylight as possible would be able to stream into the enormous first-floor entrance room of the château.

The others had already gathered there and were waiting for Jessica to join them inside. As she walked into the room, alternating large black-and-white marble tiles under her feet caused her steps to echo through the huge expanse. An enormous chandelier sparkled over her head; its numerous crystals played with the light rays passing through the windows. She marveled at the time it must take to keep them dust-free so as to playfully catch the light rays as they were now able to. There was a prism-like effect; pastel colors refracted the light through the crystals and onto the floor in spots, adding to the magical sense of whimsy of the room.

"This is the first chamber to have its renovation completed," Averi said with some satisfaction.

"Renovation?" Jessica asked.

"Yes. I have a fifteen-year plan that Dom has mapped out for the château; the plan is to go chamber by chamber to prevent any further deterioration from happening. The château wasn't as you see it now when I purchased it—no, not by any means. We started with an extensive garden restoration, which has now almost been completed. Now we need to work on the infrastructure itself. I'm also considering animating the rooms with modern technology to allow visitors to hear details of each finished project as it is completed. The entire plan will be completed at an enormous expense, of course, but by the time you finish the tour today, you will see why I consider it a worthwhile expense." Averi's own animation grew as he spoke to them; his hands were never still, and he gesticulated toward all points leading out in different directions from the entryway to stress his intention.

"Perhaps I should proceed to show our guests the château while you meet with your architects, M. Averi?" Roberts quietly asked his boss.

Jessica suddenly wondered how often Roberts was likely to offer a restraining hand on his boss.

"Yes, yes, Dom. Carry on. Why don't you? Please, make yourselves at home as Dom leads you about." Averi gracefully exited behind a private door and left Jessica and Alain alone with Roberts.

"Shall we start then?" Roberts asked as he began to take Jessica and Alain through the seemingly never-ending series of rooms, each more elaborately furnished than the previous one with period furniture, alabaster statuary, and artwork that covered the walls as well as being painted directly on the ceilings. The tour seemed to go on without end.

Room after room connected with each other via passageways, and the first and second floors were connected by stairways that only added to the sense that they would be spending much of the day attempting to take in all that was on offer. But even Averi's and Roberts's enthusiasm for their cherished château couldn't mask the underlying signs of decay, which suggested to Jessica that, without huge influxes of money, the extensive size of the building would cause it to continually slide into ruin despite Averi's description as a "worthwhile expense."

In many places the wallpaper was peeling and the carpets were in need of repair, their threads piteously straining to hold together the covering of the splintered wood beneath them. Even the gilded furnishings, although obviously originally of high quality, looked as though a skilled restorer was needed to return them to their former glory. Glancing around, Jessica thought that Averi had been hopelessly optimistic in quoting a fifteen-year plan. A twenty-five- or thirty-year plan was more likely to be necessary to complete everything that needed to be accomplished.

When they finally reached the wine caves underneath the château, the cold and dampness below ground caused a shiver to run down Jessica's neck. But she knew it wasn't just the chilliness of the space that provoked the unpleasant physical sensation in her body; there was something disturbingly depressing about the sorry need to stem the decay. It was evident even in the installed wine cellars. What a waste that such excessive amounts of cash could be spent on so many other things so much more beneficial to the average man or woman, she thought. So it was when Roberts led them up and out of the caves and into the fresh air above to finally tour the gardens that Jessica breathed a deep sigh of relief and gulped in the fragrant, clean breezes around her with gratitude.

The gardens were voluminous and appeared even more impressive up close than they had been when viewed from high above in the helicopter on their arrival. The fine gravel of the walking pathways crunched under their feet as the three inspected the many varieties of planted boxwoods and yews on view for their inspection. The trees were lined up in majestic rows, leading away from the château and back toward the woods surrounding the estate.

Finally, Roberts seemed content that he had given the guests the tour that M. Averi had commanded of him, and he then led Jessica and Alain back to the helicopter that was waiting for them in the courtyard behind the château. The pilot was still there, patiently in attendance to return them to Paris whenever they wished.

Before Roberts left them, he handed Jessica his embossed

business card. "Call me if either of you wish another tour at any time. Don't be shy about that. I can't imagine M. Averi having a problem with it. I visit the château at least once weekly to handle issues that don't require M. Averi's immediate attention, and I can arrange to bring you back by the same route. It wouldn't be a problem at all for me either." He waved to them as Jessica and Alain climbed back into their seats in the helicopter.

As the pilot checked the helicopter for takeoff and before the sounds of its whirling blades would prevent any private conversation between the two, Jessica whispered to Alain, "Did you have the same thought I did? What do you think?"

"About the château?" Alain questioned.

"Yes, about the château."

"Well, if you were thinking what a money pit—"

"Exactly!"

"Then, yes, I did."

"So do you think this is what might be the hungry baby driving a thirst for profits—if there is one—at Averi Industries?"

"It's possible," Alain noted.

"Only possible?"

"Maybe probable."

"Okay, I'm satisfied. I'll take that as a yes," Jessica said. "Then we're thinking as one mind."

"We do from time to time, you know," Alain said with a gentle smile, placing his hand on her arm, this time without any restraint.

"What's next do you think?"

"We go back to Paris. And we find a way to get a look at those numbers Mason was so interested in."

9

A Plan Is Hatched

Jessica returned to her apartment, and Alain left to pick up Odette from her friend Marie's house. Jessica still felt slightly disoriented from the helicopter ride from La Défense to Averi's château and back again to Paris. Her mind seemed to be in a haze, consumed with thoughts of how best to obtain the financial information they needed from the museum's records. The visit to Averi's château had only added fuel to the fire in her breast that Averi Industries was being used as the source of funds running the château's financially demanding machinery. Once again, though, some pangs of guilt pulsed through her heart, knowing that there was no way Alain's daughter, Odette, wouldn't be dragged further into any plan. But access to the museum was the only viable entry point for any further investigation into what irregularities might be in play. So she didn't see how it could be avoided.

Jessica pulled the key to her apartment out of her purse. Almost as soon as she opened the door, she heard her cell phone ring; it incessantly pinged as she groped into the deeper recesses of her bag for the device. She managed to extract it before the very last peal, and she plunked down into the chair nearest the entrance to the apartment after slamming the door shut with her foot in irritation.

A deep voice spoke out of the phone, but it wasn't Alain. "Hello, Jessica. It's Tom from New York. How's it going there? Any news to give me yet?"

"Before we talk, Tom, I want to ask: How's Lucy doing? Is she feeling any better?"

"Ah, Jessica darling, thanks for asking. She's as well as I could hope, but I think she's starting to come back to being more like the sister I know and love. I guess time is having a beneficial effect on her."

"Oh, Tom, I'm so glad to hear it. That's really wonderful. It makes me happy."

"Yes, it's still going to be a bit of a process with her needing to accept the new reality, but I think she's making fairly good progress at it." He paused a moment and then said, "So tell me … What's been happening on your end? Any progress of your own? I must admit I'm not as angry about everything as I was when we last spoke. So I guess that's why I haven't jumped to call you. As Lucy's been feeling better, I held off for a while.

"What I'm trying to say, Jessica, is that if you feel that I sent you on a wild goose chase or that you've had difficulty playing advance scout for me, consider this call as notice that you can come home if you'd rather. It wasn't really fair that I dropped my problem into your lap."

"Tom, I can't do that *now*."

"Why? Have you come up with something? That changes things."

"Not really, or, at least, not anything I or Alain can pigeon-hole as important to what you hoped for me to find. But, Tom, I should let you know that there's been a death at the museum." She gave him a minute to process the information she had just relayed before continuing. "So far, the official theory is an employee's suicide due to overwork and stress. But the story just doesn't hold together, at least not to me or Alain, especially since it seems Mason—that was his name—might have come across some troubling financial figures during his work there."

"So there you are! My hunch may have been right on target after all. Look, Jessica, don't they have any investigators working the case over there in Paris?"

"Yes, they do, as a matter of fact. Someone named Inspector Lanier has been assigned to the case. Alain thinks he's on the up-and-up but also probably under a good deal of political pressure to prevent any unnecessary scandal from getting attached to the name of such a powerful man like Averi. You can imagine how it is. It seems we've stepped on a bit of a hornet's nest."

"Isn't that always the case, darling, for anything that's worthwhile?"

"Yes, I guess it is. So, Tom, that's why I'm staying now. It's not just for you and Lucy any more, although you know how much I care about you and about her. I really do. It's just that I've got to make the same effort to try and find out what's been going on, now for Mason's sake as well. I didn't know him personally, although I met him briefly. But if someone harmed him, I don't want that person or persons to get away with it. I just don't. Besides, Odette has been traumatized by his death, and she needs some closure of all this mess. The only way for that to happen is for whoever may have caused this tragedy to get the punishment they deserve."

"So what are you going to do?"

"Well, Alain and I decided we've got to get at those figures Mason was concerned about. We hit a blind alley that we initially thought would lead to some answers for us with a man Mason had consulted about them. But we'll find another path,

and we'll get at them another way. We just have to be determined, that's all. You know I am, and if there's one thing Alain
is, it's determined. Once he smells something fishy, he's on the
hunt. In that way, you two are a lot alike."

"Well, thanks. That sounds like a compliment to me, and
I'll take it. Let me know as soon as you know anything further."

"Will do. Now, you just focus on your end on taking care
of Lucy."

Jessica left her apartment building and began walking toward
the Arc de Triomphe to take the metro. She was en route to the
apartment where she was to meet Alain and Odette to hash out
next steps. She admitted to herself that she was feeling somewhat uncomfortable about the prospect. It wasn't that she was
anxious about planning the next moves of the investigation that
was starting to take form. No, in fact, as she had told Tom, she
was eager to proceed with it. It was just that tonight's setting,
being the home of Alain's ex-wife and her new husband, who
were both still away from Paris on vacation, was unnerving her.

Alain had assured her that she needn't have any qualms
about being there, but she couldn't help feeling awkward. Her
hands were restless as she straightened her tousled hair. It was
being blown about her face by the wind buffeting her as she
navigated the steps down to the metro station. The sounds and
smells of the city's activity now hit her less as reassuring signs
of daily life and more as annoyances, impeding her needed
concentration. She wanted to be focused, not only on getting to
her destination but on not making any errors by crossing any
invisible boundaries, especially with respect to Odette.

The home of Josephine and Claude Dabry was situated in

Vincennes, the leafy eastern suburb of Paris. Claude Dabry was a financier, so Jessica fully expected the apartment to be an elegant one. Jessica had insisted that she make the journey by metro on her own because she wanted to limit Alain's time away from Odette.

As she exited the station at the Château de Vincennes, she pondered the irony that the locale was also the site of a medieval dungeon. Had that fact, in some bizarre way, contributed to the choice of locale for the evening's work, or was it merely a coincidental convenience? She had pondered Alain's possible ironic streak before at the Panthéon, but maybe she was just over diagnosing irony in another as a reflection of her own appreciation of the absurd. Looking around her, she had to admit the area was totally charming with its tree-lined streets, and as she neared the address Alain had given her, she mentally played with her customary idea of being a local resident herself.

After a few minutes of wandering back and forth and asking for directions several times, she finally found the apartment building where Alain and Odette were waiting for her arrival and went inside. The building was a more modern one than the location of her own sublet. This one was sandwiched between two older buildings and looked as though it had only recently replaced a prior version of itself. In this building no concierge like Madame Clair was likely to be found, but Jessica was consoled by the sleek, efficient elevator that took her up to the fourth floor with no need for her to mount any stairs. She didn't want to take a chance of looking any more exhausted and disheveled from the climb than she likely appeared from her already having circumnavigated Vincennes a few times.

As the elevator door opened, she immediately caught sight of Odette hanging out of the door to her apartment, expectantly waiting for her. Alain's daughter's eagerness to see her arrive alleviated some of Jessica's anxiety at overstepping her place with Odette. Now the girl looked every bit the Parisian teenager without the professional museum attire Jessica had last seen her wearing. Odette was in jeans, a short black T-shirt, and flip-flops. Jessica was happy to see that Odette's face was no longer distorted by the anguished lines that Alain had described the girl as having had before; it appeared that, like Lucy, time itself was working its healing magic on this young woman.

"Hello, Odette. Did I keep you waiting long?" Jessica asked, coming up to her. She decided to hold back on *la bise*, still not sure whether two kisses on the cheek would be appropriate. Jessica felt she must have handled it correctly because it seemed Odette took no offense at any lapse in customary practice.

"No. No. Come in. Papa's inside. This time we just ordered pizza from a shop I like, but I really think Papa was afraid of using the kitchen here. Don't take this the wrong way, but it's a lot more complicated than the one in your apartment." She laughed, and Jessica was struck by the sweetness of her smile, now freed of the stress and anxiety of personal loss.

"No offense taken. I'm fully aware that cooking isn't one of my strong points."

Jessica stepped inside and, for just a minute, thought she had been transported to a space station. The apartment's walls were stark white without any hint of color to break the whiteness, and black industrial track lighting ran across the lengths of the high ceilings. The furnishings were low to the floor without patterned fabric to brighten them; each seat was covered in black or white leather, and tables were made of metal and glass. Yet somehow, the arrangement all managed to hang together and showed that whoever had chosen the obviously expensive pieces possessed a sense of good taste.

"Comfy, isn't it?" Alain asked, entering the room. "My ex-wife's husband is a more modern man than I am, I guess."

"So I gather. But I kind of like it."

"Odette explained that I thought it best we avoid the appliances in the kitchen? The last thing we want to do is knock any one of them out of commission."

"She did, indeed, explain the situation."

"Good. Then let's have the pizza before it gets cold. It arrived just before you got here."

The three sat down around the huge dining room table that was constructed of marble, brass, and wood—the only more traditional materials visible in the entire apartment that Jessica had seen so far—as Odette played hostess. As Odette graciously served the meal, Jessica had another chance to witness the relaxed interaction between father and daughter as they tried to come up with a viable plan of action to go forward with.

"The obvious thing that needs to be done first is to get a copy of what Mason had been looking at before his … death," Jessica said, hoping the last word wouldn't once again upset Odette. The girl seemed so content playing hostess, and Jessica was leery of upsetting the boat in any way with an awkward word, so she treaded softly. "I'm just not confident that even if we can get at them, we'll know how to interpret the numbers. I like to think I'm good at math—but not that good. And I certainly have no background in art estimation other than what I've learned from buying some pieces for myself here and there. Or, in some cases, I have gotten them as gifts," she added.

She thought back momentarily to her favorite painting, which Alain had given her after they had solved a mystery at the art fair in Miami and which still hung proudly over her office desk at home in Connecticut. The picture was one that she often looked at with tenderness; it had seemed in some small way to be a link between them, even apart from each other.

"You mean you didn't learn that skill during our last escapade at the art fair?" Alain was obviously on the same page. "I would have thought you would have."

"Very funny, but no."

"Well, don't worry. We've got that covered." He looked at Odette and said to his daughter, "Go on. Tell her."

"Do you remember my friend Marie whom I stayed with when you and Papa went to M. Averi's château?" Without waiting for a response from Jessica, Odette continued with the same determined expression her father so often displayed. "Marie's father is an accountant. He's willing to help. Papa already spoke to him, and he knows not to mention what we plan to anyone. We just have to get him the data."

"Emmanuel Deschamps is quite good at what he does," Alain added. "He's promised to take a look at the data and give us an honest assessment. And Marie is a trustworthy friend to Odette. I don't think she'll say anything to anyone. There's no need to worry about either of them. On that I think we can count."

"So now we just have to figure out how to get at those figures from the museum," Jessica said, tapping her forefinger to her temple.

"That's also not a problem," Odette said, again looking just like her father, Jessica thought. "I think I have some idea what Mason was looking at. I don't think anyone knows that Mason transferred a lot of his data to my computer so that I could help with some of the easy items if he needed me to. But maybe he wanted a backup? I guess we'll never know." She seemed to drift off in her concentration for a moment before continuing. "Because of the security system, I just can't get into the file except from inside the museum. And I'm sure Aleixo will let us in when no one's around, so we can take a peek. Louis I'm not as sure of," she added with the first hint of doubt that Jessica could detect.

"That's settled then," Alain said. "For now, let's eat up. Tomorrow we'll get into the museum if Aleixo's as good as you say, Odette. Then we'll get at those figures and see what Marie's father thinks about them." He reached across the table and placed his muscular hand upon his daughter's thin wrist before saying with more seriousness, "That way we'll know if Mason found something that someone didn't want him to find out about."

10

A Return to Musée Averi

Only a few spare lights were on, which shone through the windows of the museum, as Jessica, Alain, and Odette quietly approached the employee entrance of Musée Averi. The early morning darkness still tenaciously lingered against the broad sides of the building, adding to the aura of absolute desertion, which the stark walls and unlit lampposts beside them complemented. True to her assurances from the night before, Odette had pulled a reluctant Aleixo into their plan. The security guard had grudgingly agreed to provide them access, and only access, to the museum at that early hour. No further assistance had been offered.

"Let's hope Aleixo is as good as his word and will let us in," Jessica said, traces of doubt creeping into her voice.

"Don't worry," Odette said confidently. "Aleixo promised he would be here extra early to let us in so Louis doesn't have to be involved in any way. I know we can trust Aleixo. I know we can."

At that very moment, the security guard appeared from behind the entrance door, looking somewhat disheveled, which Jessica ascribed to his being on duty much earlier than usual for him. She saw him cast an ill-disposed, suspicious eye at her and Alain as he said in French, "Odette, I thought you would be alone."

"Aleixo, you must know that I had to have them here with me," Odette said pleadingly. "I can't do what I need to do all by myself. You must know that!"

"Okay, okay. It's fine. I'm not mad. Just don't make any noise, that's all. The last thing I need is for Louis to hear us if he comes in early." Aleixo practically pushed them all inside. Then he immediately disappeared from view, making it clear he wanted no further part of the whole operation and was already regretting his prior acquiescence to the plan.

Odette led the way back through the museum to the office Jessica and Alain had first visited when Mason was still working so diligently at his desk. Odette switched on the lights. Jessica thought how empty the room now looked, devoid of its former dedicated occupant. It was as though there was a tangible void in Mason's previous work space that was more than the empty surface and had been assiduously wiped clean of all the papers and meager personal items that had once belonged to its prior occupant. It seemed so sad.

"Let's get started," Alain said, bringing Jessica's mind back to their purpose for being there. "Aleixo obviously isn't comfortable with this, and I'm even less certain of Louis, so let's not waste any more time than we have to. Come on."

Odette sat down in front of her computer, while Jessica and Alain hovered just behind her back to watch her at work. Concentration and determination were expressed in her furrowed brow and were reflected in the mirrored surface of the computer screen in front of her. The teenager painstakingly reviewed file after file until she finally found what she was trying so earnestly to retrieve from the computer.

With newfound mastery in her voice, she said, "Here it is.

I remember now. Mason said something about it, and the way he said it I thought funny at the time. But now maybe it all makes sense."

"What did he say?" Alain asked.

"He said something like: 'I may need you to help me with this but not just yet. I want to be sure I'm on the right track. I don't want to involve you if I don't need to.' But then I forgot about exactly what he had said, even when he mentioned it later on. I just remembered now how he looked when he first said it—as though the file puzzled him more than anything else. Isn't memory a funny thing?"

"Was the file titled in some way?" Jessica asked.

"It may have been, but unfortunately, I always retitle my files so I'll be able to find them more easily. I've learned that's the best way for me to keep things organized. I like to be organized."

"Well, at least you did find it. But are you sure it's the right one?"

"Yes. Definitely!" She started transferring the file to a flash drive she had pulled out of the side pocket of her jeans.

Jessica was worried the sound of her beating heart could be heard as she and Alain watched Odette work.

Barely a minute later, there was a noise outside the door to the office.

"Are you done yet?" Jessica asked, anxiety starting to raise the pitch of her voice even in a whisper.

"Just a minute," Odette answered calmly, continuing to transfer the file to the flash drive.

The door handle started to turn as three pairs of eyes focused on the chrome knob. Jessica held her breath until Odette completed the transfer and stashed the flash drive back in her pocket just as the door opened. Jessica was finally able to let the air out of her lungs with a deep sigh of relief when she saw that it was only Aleixo standing in front of the open door, his large form backlit by the now illuminated hallway.

"Are you finished yet?" he asked impatiently, just as Jessica had done before, worry lines evident and distorting the guard's face. "Louis is here, and he keeps thinking he hears noises in the museum. I can't distract him for much longer. He's getting suspicious. I need you all to leave *now*, or I'm going to lose my job."

"We're going right now. Don't worry. Thanks, Aleixo." Odette went up to him and planted a demure kiss on each of his cheeks, which seemed to immediately mollify him. A few minutes later, after checking the hallway left and right to assure there was still no sign of Louis, he guided them back out of the exit from which they had come so that he could return to his post and the security of his unendangered job.

Emmanuel Deschamps's corporate accounting firm was located in La Défense. It was situated not far from the headquarters of Averi Industries. Jessica couldn't help but ponder the coincidence of the fact that the two locations were so close together. But as luck would have it, Averi Industries was not one of Deschamps's many clients. Because of that, Marie's father had said he felt absolutely no conflict of interest in helping out his daughter's friend as he planned to do; he would use his accounting skills to give his new acquaintances the benefit of his many years of experience at analyzing corporate financial accounts.

His office was in a high-tech, modern building, similar to that of Averi Industries, but of somewhat less celebrity.

Unlike the other office Jessica and Alain had recently visited, Deschamps's place of work had no security guards on site to screen visitors upon entry; Jessica and Alain were merely instructed by the young woman at the reception desk to head on up to the sixth floor to find M. Deschamps on their own.

There, they were met by the experienced accountant himself. He was a middle-aged man. He was slightly balding on the crown of his head and wore thick reading glasses, which looked as though they had helped M. Deschamps through university, examinations, and the business knowledge he needed to obtain to achieve his current level of success. They dangled from the bridge of his nose as he peered over the top of the glasses at the two new arrivals. Odette had informed Jessica and Alain that the parents of many of Marie's friends had gone to him for accounting assistance whenever needed, and it was always graciously given without any hesitation.

"Now, let me see what you have here for me," Deschamps directed, having previously been instructed he would need to discuss his analysis in English, in which he was luckily fluent. The three were installed in the seclusion of his private office; he wasn't the type to waste any time on pleasantries.

Alain promptly handed over Odette's flash drive, which she had grudgingly relinquished to her father after being told that it was perhaps better if he and Jessica met with Emmanuel by themselves. Deschamps immediately hooked up the drive to the computer on his desk and soon pulled up the relevant figures on the computer screen in front of him. He sat silently studying them for a good fifteen minutes, only occasionally clicking his tongue against the roof of his mouth, as though in exasperation that his computer wasn't able to keep up with the quickness of his mind.

Finally, he removed his glasses from the tip of his nose and

11

The Inspectors Confer

Jessica and Alain sat on one side of the large desk in the detective's office at the Police Judiciaire. The stone-faced Inspector Georges Lanier sat on the other. To Lanier's right stood his younger partner, Inspector Jules Pecor. Jessica watched Pecor listen intently to the exchange between Lanier and Alain. At various times in the discourse, the young man's expression changed, intermittently showing consternation as he appeared to mentally follow the financial details rattled off by Alain to Lanier. But as the older detective listened to Alain explicitly detail the financial irregularities Deschamps had gleaned from Mason Henri's files, Lanier's bushy eyebrows and the muscles around his mouth didn't move at all.

But Lanier was closely following every point his Canadian counterpart was making, of that Jessica was sure. From the moment Alain began to speak, Lanier's eyes remained steadfastly fixed on him; the French detective hadn't once shifted the position of his burly body, and his coffee mug sat untouched, the steam from the cup having long ago dissipated since it was first plopped down on the top of the desk when he came into the room.

"I see," Lanier said curtly once Alain finished talking. "I

must admit it does look convenient for M. Henri to have been overtaken with such stress and strain that he felt the need to end his life just as he is examining the *irregularities* you have found."

Jessica wasn't sure if she detected sarcasm in the tone of the detective's voice. She didn't expect it from him now; his manner seemed so deadpan. She quickly looked to Alain to see if his reaction would give her any clue as to his counterpart's intent, but he just looked his usual enigmatic self when involved in these types of situations. The ability to conceal their emotions, which both men so successfully possessed and which she had never been able to own, particularly irked her. Then Jessica heard Lanier continue to speak, and she turned back to look at him.

"What I will do is to have the files reviewed here by my department. I gather M. Deschamps did you both a favor and will not wish to be further imposed upon, so I will not do so. In addition, I will need my own analysis to be conducted, so there is no further need to involve your friend. But I am not discounting what you have brought me today. On the contrary, this information makes it easier for me to pursue investigation into M. Henri's unfortunate demise without pressure being borne upon me to close it down prematurely. I previously explained to you that Frédéric Averi's name carries a lot of weight in this country—and, indeed, it also does so around the world. But I guess that is the way it always is."

Jessica heard the inspector's soft sigh and reasoned his last statement was primarily made to himself. She wondered how many other cases he had pursued over the years and how many he had been pressured to close down prematurely. His words rang a bell of similarity to those of Tom's, who was also well versed in the complexity of political expediency.

"I will contact you as soon as I have the confirmation I need," Lanier added. "Sometimes experience is better than the wish to be useful." He stood up from his desk and, as abruptly as he had come in, dismissed them.

As Jessica and Alain left the office, Jessica again pondered the similarity of Lanier's last words, this time to those of Jacques Charles who had uttered them about Mason Henri's quest to probe the finances of the Musée Averi. She could only hope that Inspector Lanier would prove to be more of a help to them than Jacques Charles had been.

"So what's bothering you?" Alain asked.

Jessica and Alain were having lunch at a small bistro not far from the Police Judiciaire after having provided Lanier with Odette's flash drive containing Mason Henri's file.

"I'm just not sure we should have left everything we had in Lanier's hands ... That's all. I'm still not certain if I totally trust him. He's another one who's very hard to read."

"To whom are you comparing him?"

"To Jacques Charles, of course."

"Oh. Well we had no choice, Jessica. Besides, I think Lanier will do the right thing in the end."

"You do? Good, because I'm not so sure myself."

"I know your keen investigative mind must be working in total overdrive by now, but remember, Lanier does this for a living," Alain said firmly. "It's his job, after all."

"You inspectors all stick together, don't you, though? It's rather annoying."

"We have to. That's an important lesson I've learned over the years. In any case, I have a good feeling about him. Trust my instincts, why don't you? They're not bad, you know."

"I do trust them. You know that. I guess you may be right. So then, what do you suggest do we do now?" Jessica questioned.

"Do now? We wait, of course," he replied. "I understand that's a hard thing for you to do."

"It's not only the waiting that I find difficult. I just feel that if Lanier confirms some financial shenanigans and even if he finds out more than we suspected was there, he'll ultimately fail to tie it to Mason's death. I just don't want the killer—if there is one, I know, I know—to get off."

"So what do *you* want to be done?"

"I haven't figured that out yet. But believe me, I'll think of something. And when I do, you'll be the very first to know."

Once home and on her own again, Jessica reached a clear decision; uncertainty no longer clouded her brain. She knew it was time to act. She wasn't content, like Alain, to sit and wait for Inspector Lanier to do his job. She was mulling over her thoughts in the kitchen of her Parisian apartment, which was now beginning to feel more and more to her like a home. The window of the kitchen in the back of the apartment looked out onto the small courtyard behind the building. It was a charming spot, graced with ornamental trees, patches of green grass, and variegated flowers, and there were a couple of wooden benches just begging to be sat upon so the spot could be appreciated in calm solitude. She was sure that Madame Clair saw to it that the gardener who tended the plot once weekly did not neglect any area because she had occasionally heard them arguing with each other over the appearance of one or another of the flower beds and how they should be tended. With its view of the pretty garden, the kitchen was a good place to think.

Jessica got up from the kitchen chair and went over to stand by the window and enjoy the view. As she looked down at the garden below, she noticed that the putty around the kitchen window frame had worn away in several spots, mainly along the long edge of the window. In a few places there was flaking of the soft gray putty, which freely crumbled away in her hands as she rubbed at it. The window frame also had an area of rot running along the length of one side, and when she pushed against it, she felt the window shift slightly in its wooden framing. She would have to make Madame Clair aware of it so it could be repaired.

She gathered the concierge would be able to arrange for it to be done expediently. She seemed so efficient, and Jessica was a little surprised Madame Clair hadn't already noticed it. Perhaps the woman's eyesight wasn't that sharp any longer. The thought brought her mind back to the wooden bannister of the upstairs gallery at Musée Averi that had seemed too delicate for its purpose and what Mason's body must have looked like once it hit the marble floor below. Alain had spared her most of the details, and she was grateful for that, but she wished he had been as easily able to spare Odette the personal vision of it. She shivered slightly at the thought.

"Well, I'm just not in the mood to hang around and play the tourist," she said out loud, leaving the kitchen behind her. She went into the bedroom and got out her cell phone and the business card Dom Roberts had handed to her at the visit to Averi's château in the countryside. She dialed the number on the card and in seconds was gratified to hear the call connect.

"Bonjour?"

"Monsieur Roberts?" she asked.

"Oui," he replied.

"This is Jessica Shepard."

"Hello. Don't tell me you are ready to tour Château Averi

again so soon. It would be a pleasure for me to be your guide once more. I always enjoy showing the château several times to new people. It often takes more than one viewing to fully appreciate it. But I must admit, I was not expecting to hear from you so soon as this."

"No. It isn't that. I appreciate your kind offer, but I'm not yet ready for another visit. But I would like a word with you, at your convenience, of course."

"Yes. That would not be a problem. But may I ask what it is about?" he questioned.

"You know, I would rather discuss it when we meet," she said.

"That is fine, if you would rather. But from your reticence, I assume neither the office in La Défense or at the museum is an appropriate place to talk. May I suggest another spot then?"

"I think that would be a good idea."

"Excellent. There is a favorite bistro of mine down the avenue from the museum. You are sure to find it, as it is the only one on the block. I will be able to meet you there in about one hour. That would be most convenient for me because after I can go to the museum to do some work. Would that be convenient for you to meet me there?"

"Perfect. I'll see you there. Goodbye."

Jessica hung up the phone, satisfied that she was able to set up the meeting so easily. Now she had one hour to get her thoughts in order before she met him. Something inside her told her it wasn't just a case of nepotism, which Emmanuel Deschamps had alluded to, that had led to the linkage of Dom Roberts and Jacques Charles to Averi Industries. There was more going on there. She felt it. She just needed to parse it out with one or another of them. And between the two, she thought she would have an easier time of it with Roberts than with

Charles. Somehow the older man seemed more of an enigma.
For now, she would leave Alain out of the mix; she knew he
wouldn't like it, but she'd have to risk it. It would be the price
he would have to pay for being so complacent. She was still
annoyed at the way his feathers never seemed to get ruffled.

She threw her cell phone and Roberts's business card back
into her purse, grabbed a light jacket, and left the apartment to
meet him. As she headed out the door, she thought with a shrug
that this was working out to be the next interesting phase of yet
one more of her investigative adventures.

12

Roberts Explains

When Jessica entered the small bistro down the avenue from Musée Averi, she saw that Roberts was already there. He was seated at a table by himself. She still wasn't sure how she would frame the borders of their conversation, but her general plan was to use him as a type of tour guide. This time not as one to the inner parts of Averi's château but instead to the intricacies of Averi Industries, which would otherwise be off-limits to her. If she could just manage to fathom the depths of Averi's vast holdings, which she already knew ran the gamut of grand château and private art museum, as well as many diverse companies, like the one doing the genetic testing that Lucy had relied upon, then everything would hopefully fall into place, and the best way forward would present itself.

She approached his table feeling as though she was a gladiator entering the arena for two-person, hand-to-hand combat. He saw her almost immediately and got up, pulling out the chair across from him for her to sit down upon. It was a polite gesture that only momentarily disarmed her.

"I'm glad you were able to find this place," Roberts said, sitting back down. I suggested meeting here because it seemed appropriate for a private discussion. The waiters know not to

disturb their customers unless they're summoned. Although, I
must admit I'm a little confused as to what it could be that you
wished to discuss in confidence, considering our relatively brief
acquaintance with each other."

"I'm sorry. I didn't mean to sound at all mysterious when
I spoke to you on the phone," Jessica began. "That wasn't my
intention. But you're right. What I wanted to talk about does
involve a private matter—though not one involving me exactly.
It actually involves a friend of mine, and in order to help, I first
need to understand Frédéric Averi's companies a little better."

"How so? I still don't really comprehend you and what information you're looking to ascertain. I'm not sure what I can
tell you that is much different from what you learned when you
came to meet M. Averi himself at the office in La Défense. It
must have been obvious that Averi Industries is a global corporation with many holdings around the world. Certainly, an
internet search would provide any additional information that
might interest you."

"Yes. But there are some things that are only better understood through person-to-person interaction. Don't you think
so? For instance, why would a man who manages such a vast
network of global companies, including one that I've learned
does genetic testing, also involve himself to such a degree with
an art museum and a vast château, which I gather he's planning
to make into a popular tourist destination from what I saw when
I was there?"

"But is that really so hard to understand? Come now. Great
men like M. Averi enjoy involving themselves in many great
things. It is anything but uncommon, I think."

Jessica wondered, for only a moment, whether Roberts was
mocking her, but then she couldn't fail to notice the way his eyes
gleamed with admiration at the mention of his employer. Were

his eyes actually tearing up? She wasn't sure, but she thought he seemed to be serious and not sarcastic at all.

"Well, let me put it another way," she said, deciding to follow his lead. "How can he know that each and every one of these *great things*, as you say, are being managed properly, if they are so extensive?"

"Excuse me?"

"I didn't mean to imply anything nefarious. Just that it must be hard for such a busy man to keep a clear and keen eye on so much, in so many places."

"*Nefarious* did you say?" Roberts asked.

Jessica suddenly felt a blow had hit home across the table. She had been proceeding by the seat of her pants. But at that moment, she knew the best way to elicit unguarded information from Roberts was to trigger his highly protective instincts toward Averi Industries and toward Averi himself. It was the only weapon she had.

"Jessica, I can only guess what you are alluding to. Mason Henri's death was an extremely unfortunate event." He practically spat out the words. No more was he the polite, solicitous companion to grab a bite with. "But it shouldn't detract from the fact that the museum is a gift to all who enter its doors. The art is of the highest quality—a true testament to what Averi Industries has achieved for the world. And once brought back to its original glory, Château Averi will be an even greater testament to the man and to his corporation. Averi Industries creates many beneficial products; the genetic testing component is just in its infancy and is only a part of them. But it and numerous other operations will not only benefit many but will also generate enormous funds to bankroll the never-ending amounts needed for the renovation of Averi's magnificent château—"

Suddenly, Roberts stopped talking, but his mouth was still

open, almost gaping, as though his mind had finally caught up with his unbridled emotions. He slowly pulled a white linen handkerchief out of his pants pocket and methodically wiped the edges of his lips, where a few drops of spittle that had spewed out of them still lingered.

Jessica could feel he was using the maneuver to control his emotions. She then watched him visibly relax his lean shoulders as he moved them from side to side, and he sank back into his chair. He suddenly looked fatigued, as if their conversation had drained him of some vigor. But Jessica couldn't be sure if she was misreading the signs. She knew she had a tendency to rapidly convert signs into symptoms. It was a residuum of her many years of medical training.

"I think I see what you mean," Jessica said, now deciding to take down the heat of the moment a few degrees. She had learned from Alain when to apply the pressure and when it made more sense to release it. "Anyway, you must have so much to do, and I think that I've taken up enough of your time already."

"Yes. Yes, I do," he said almost gratefully. "Perhaps we can meet another time if you have any further questions. I think that would be preferable."

"That would be lovely. Then excuse me if I leave you now."

"But next time we must actually break bread." He gesticulated to the empty table in front of them, on which there were still only two empty glasses and two settings of cutlery.

"Agreed," Jessica said, and she quickly got up and left the bistro.

Once out of sight, Jessica started to walk over to the Parc Monceau. It was the closest park around, and she wanted to be outside in the fresh air after having spoken to Roberts. She needed to clear her head and think about what she had just gleaned from her meeting with him in that stuffy bistro. For the first time, she regretted her selfish impulse to sound him out on her own; now she wished she had Alain's steadfast evaluative skills on hand to serve as a counterbalance to her more intuitive impressions. But it was too late for that. She had wanted to handle this by herself, and now it was what it was. She would have to wait to get Alain's take on what Roberts had said after the fact—if she had the temerity to let Alain know she had kept him out of the loop and plowed forward on her own.

And what was it that Roberts had told her? Only that he had confirmed Averi's château was of paramount importance to its owner. Was that really so unexpected? Wasn't that what Roberts had said? But on the other hand, had the vast money pit become some kind of divine goddess that the two men needed to serve above all else? And was their devotion forcing them to demand such huge profits from Averi's holdings that best practices were being thrown to the winds? Even worse, might Mason have come to the same conclusion as she had and been taken off the scent ... by whatever means necessary? Or was she merely overreading Roberts's dedication as a loyal employee to the corporation he served.

Her thoughts flashed through her mind in such rapid succession that she almost failed to notice she had finally reached her destination—the park. She went through the gates and found a free bench to sit down. She suddenly felt some of the fatigue that Roberts had seemed to display at the end of their talk. The mental gymnastics was taking a surprisingly physical toll on her body. She watched as a few joggers ran by on the curving paths around her. She envied their lack of concern as they sprinted by her, joking and conversing with each other. They seemed so carefree, which, at the moment, she felt anything but.

Indecision now assailed her. Was now a good time to confer

with Alain? She still hesitated before calling him and thought for a minute. Even if he weren't annoyed at her cornering Roberts on her own, he would just tell her politely that she should have waited for Lanier's report. And maybe she should have. After all, had she learned anything worthwhile, or had she just raised Roberts's suspicions when she needn't have—if he was even actually involved in the first place?

Then it came to her like a bolt of lightning, despite the fair weather around her. Tom Martine had started her down this difficult road, and it was so unlike him to totally delegate an assignment to someone else, even one he knew well and trusted. He must have done some of his own research by now. She just knew it. He was an excellent journalist, after all.

For the first time, she was angry—angry at herself, angry at him, and angry at the situation she was now in. It didn't make any sense that Tom wasn't looking into Averi Industries himself. If she knew him as well as she thought she did, he was waiting cautiously, gathering his facts, and would only let her in on them when he was good and ready—and on his own timetable. Well, it was time for her to turn the tables on him and get *him* to do some of her legwork.

She jerked her cell phone out of her purse, pulling it out so violently that she nearly dropped it on the floor. After valiantly catching the spinning device in her lap and turning it on, instead of dialing Alain, she dialed Tom, tapping out the numbers as forcefully as she could to release the remnants of her own frustration onto the digital device.

The connection went through smoothly, despite her attack on her cell phone, and she heard Tom's deep voice on the other end of the line. This time he wasn't going to charm her by any means. She wasn't going to give him any chance for that. She was going to get some answers out of him—and now.

"Hello, darling. Any news?" he asked with his usual bantering tone.

"Tom, I'm not doing the talking just yet. I think it's time for *you* to do the talking. What do *you* know about Averi Industries?" She purposely let her annoyance with him resonate in the sound of her voice.

He must have understood her frustration because she heard him take a breath before he spoke. "All right. You got me, and you know me so well. I have been doing some of my own research, and I should have shared it with you. It was wrong of me. I can tell you're angry. I'm sorry, and I'll make it up to you now. I have been thinking about this nonstop, believe me. Look. If someone has been working the numbers to their own advantage at that museum—and if we don't know yet who's putting the pen to the paper—someone else has got to be on the receiving end of it. It's the only thing that makes sense. There would be no point otherwise. I figured it has to be an insurance company or, at the very least, an art buyer. Anyway, I did some digging, and I came up with a name for you."

"Who did you find?"

"Gabriel Maes."

"Who's he?" she asked. "I've never heard of him—at least not that I can remember."

"Well, I didn't expect you to, darling," he told her.

Jessica could tell from his voice that he knew he had her again.

"Neither did I until I did some digging around. You know me. I can be a pretty good scavenger when the need arises. It's part of my charm. You know, like the prisoner of war who always manages to find just what's needed for his unit's escape. Anyway, back to the point. Maes is a highly successful diamond dealer with enough funds to let him indulge his love of art, and he's been buying art—and a lot of it, I should add—which Musée Averi unloads from time to time. But there's one small catch. You know there's always one. Nothing is ever that easy."

"What's that?" Jessica asked, almost afraid to hear the answer.

"He's based in Antwerp."

"Antwerp? In Belgium?"

"Jessica, you know your geography! I'm impressed. Anyway, it's right in your neighborhood. Isn't that convenient?"

"Very funny. So I assume you're suggesting I go by myself to Antwerp and meet—"

"Gabriel Maes. Yes. But not alone, darling, of course not. I wouldn't want you traveling across Europe by yourself. What do you take me for? You know I'm a gentleman. Go get your friend, Raynaud, the tall Canadian, to chaperone you, darling."

"Oh. He'll just love doing that."

"Now, Jessica, I'm sure that he will. Don't underestimate him. That's not like you. He's a detective, isn't he? He'll do it. Ask him. He won't be able to say no to you. You'll see. I promise you that. I won't be wrong."

"Tom, you know that you could coax a timid turtle out of his shell—even without the juicy lettuce as an inducement."

"You're not a turtle, dearie. Don't be so ridiculous!"

"Thanks very much!"

"Now, you go on ahead and call Raynaud, then go see Maes in Antwerp, and only then let me know what you find out. You can wait until you're less annoyed with me. Stick to the plan, and you'll go far. It's a good plan. Bye."

13

Paris to Antwerp and Back

Jessica and Alain entered Gare du Nord station in the heart of Paris. They had left Odette to stay with the Deschamps while they were to be in Belgium. Just as Tom had predicted, with a little coaxing, Alain had come around to the idea of accompanying Jessica to Antwerp for a meeting with Maes. He had done so only after Jessica had promised that she would arrange no further solo encounters with anyone from Averi Industries—at least until they heard back from Inspector Lanier on the detective's progress with the case.

At that time of day, Gare du Nord was abuzz with human activity; innumerable travelers were rapidly scurrying from one corner of the massive station to the other. Rolling suitcases scraping against the busy concrete floors of the station and backpacks swung over people's shoulders jabbed at Jessica and Alain in every direction they turned as they moved deeper into the station.

"There's our platform," Jessica said, looking up at the large flashing sign above their heads.

Following the flow of people toward the train tracks, they melded into the crowd of other riders and then diverged with those who were also heading to the train to Antwerp. The trip was to take less than three hours. Tom had previously emailed Jessica Maes's address and had arranged for the diamond dealer to expect Jessica and Alain's arrival in his hometown.

Jessica had never been to Antwerp before. Part of her couldn't help being excited at the thought of taking the train to see the European city for the first time. She knew it was one of the busiest ports in Europe and had learned that about 70 percent of the world's diamonds were traded there. She also knew it had been home to some of the greatest Flemish painters, including Anthony van Dyck and Peter Paul Rubens, and was now considered a source of modern fashion design. But other than those bare and basic facts, the city was an enigma to her.

After she had gotten off the phone with Tom the day before, she had researched Gabriel Maes and had learned that he was a prominent, local diamond dealer, just as Tom had described. He was a man in his fifties with a business address near the Central Station and the Grote Markt, Antwerp's historic central square. His private home was farther away from the medieval center of the city. They were to meet Maes at his home and had been told the best way to get there from the station was to walk.

The train ride passed quickly. Almost before she knew it, they reached Central Station. Once outside in the open air, there could be no doubt as to why Maes would have chosen Antwerp to continue to live in. Diamond store after diamond store virtually littered their path as Jessica and Alain walked through the town toward Maes's home. Each shop window seemed to outdo the next one with the number of diamonds sparkling in the sun; the sparkle added artificial radiance to that of the beams of bright sunlight coming directly from the sky above.

As they moved farther and farther away from the central hub of the city and toward their rendezvous, the streets became less congested and more residential. Eventually, they managed to locate their destination; it was a tall, ultramodern building with striking views of the river, which would be visible from its upper floors. The glass and steel structure was a far cry from the traditional red-brick buildings they had left far behind them in the older part of town. They entered the building, and the sleek elevator rapidly took them up to the penthouse.

"Life at the top," Jessica said as the doors opened and she and Alain were deposited onto an elaborately decorated private lobby. "This isn't what I would have expected somehow."

"Why ever not?" Alain asked.

"It's just so classic compared with the exterior of the building. To me, they don't mesh together. I would have expected something more minimalist."

"Remember. Diamonds. Art. I'd have been surprised if it didn't look exactly like this."

"I guess you've had much more experience than I have had with old-world grandeur." She laughed. "Forget I ever said it." She continued looking around at the deep crimson watered-silk wallpaper covering the walls, which served as backdrop to carefully situated wall sconces above their heads. The lights served to illuminate a series of paintings, which were strategically placed about the lobby and looked to have been done in their day by a school of talented Flemish masters.

Before they had any further time to study the paintings around them, a heavy, oaken door suddenly opened, revealing an older man of extremely diminutive proportions. He was wearing a crisp white shirt and a dark suit. It flashed through Jessica's mind that he must have needed to obtain the suit in the boys' department of a clothing store to get the sizing right before she realized that this man would never purchase his clothes off the rack. Yes, there was something very commanding about his presence, despite his extremely small stature.

"Hello. You are both exactly on time," he said with perfect English diction, enunciating each word in turn. "Precision is always appreciated. I am Gabriel Maes. I was expecting you both. Please, come inside."

Further introductions were rapidly made. It was clear that Maes wished to get right down to business without further delay. He led them behind him into an elegant inner salon, which was the first entertaining room attached to the hallway. It had additional paintings hung on its walls, similarly illuminated by wall sconces as those in the penthouse lobby had been. It was also decorated in a similar style to that of the entrance lobby with silk wallpaper lining spaces that were not broken by windows.

Maes positioned his guests on an intricately carved sofa with plush upholstery between the carved frame. It was situated across from him, and from it, through the one large wall of windows, Jessica and Alain could watch boats going back and forth across the murky river in the far distance. It was a gracious room in which to conduct the business they had traveled to Antwerp to do. Jessica could only imagine what other transactions had been accomplished there and how many funds had transferred hands there, considering Maes's vocation and his obviously indulged passion for art.

"When Tom Martine reached out to me, I must tell you that I was very eager to meet his representatives in person," Maes said once they had all settled into place. "Look around my gracious home." He continued as though he'd read Jessica's thoughts. He pointed to either side of him. "It must be clear to you both that I am an aficionado of the finer things in life."

He laughed softly at his own joke and then went on speaking.

"Unfortunately, I must also admit that *sometimes* my desire to obtain works of art that I love overcomes my better business instincts, which at other times are not derelict by any means. No, it doesn't often happen, but I must admit that from time to time it does. Now, I assure you that these beautiful items you see around you are excellent. What I am getting at is that there have been *a few* times when I have made purchases that have turned out, on closer inspection, not to have had the true provenances I was led to believe."

Jessica watched Maes continue to gently stroke the lapels of his expertly tailored suit as he spoke, and she couldn't help but think that he looked as though he would be more at home in an ascot and velvet smoking jacket with satin lapels to accept the gentle stroking of his hands. She forced herself to ignore his particular gestures, as well as her roving mental images, and continue to focus on what he was saying.

"Now, you can easily understand that should such knowledge come out in the public eye, *some* might think my judgement in other things also suspect. Obviously, in my line of work that would be catastrophic to my personal business reputation. That would be unacceptable. Now, needless to say, I cannot in any way allow that unfortunate circumstance to happen."

"We have no wish to cause you any unnecessary difficulties," Alain said.

"Of course not," Jessica added.

"I am grateful for that—truly I am. On the other hand, you should both know that I do consider myself an honest man. And, as such, I do not like being cheated. I don't like the thought of others being cheated either. Now, I am a man of highly significant financial resources, which you have both most likely deduced from meeting me and making even a cursory examination of my home. So I have taken it upon myself to have drafted papers showing some *little proof* of my concerns, which might be of use to you. It was not so difficult to accomplish. I agree to provide them to you both on the strict condition that my name remains pure of any adverse publicity for the reasons I have alluded to previously."

"I think we can guarantee that we will not pass on your papers without such assurances having been obtained," Alain said.

"Good. That is exactly what Mr. Martine promised when we conversed together. Now, you may be aware that these papers might implicate Mr. Dom Roberts. I am not as squeamish about his reputation." He laughed softly again. "I will not bore you with the details of how we became acquainted."

"Obviously," Jessica said. She was getting a real taste for Maes's manner of speaking. It was beginning to have a charming ring to it.

"Suffice to say, Dom Roberts was my contact—and my sole contact—for several of my acquisitions. But I was under the impression that my purchases were made to allow the museum to acquire even more spectacular substitute acquisitions. I would not have made those purchases otherwise; I assure you both. I do like to consider myself a patron of the arts, in all the better meanings of the phrase. I do not enjoy my patronage being misused. I think that we understand each other. Do we not?"

Maes got up from his chair without waiting for a reply and went over to a large mahogany desk. It was positioned to one side of the room under yet another painting. There was a series of crystal paperweights running across the top of the desk, lined up perfectly in a row. Each of the glass figures shook slightly as the diamond dealer carefully seated himself in another chair in front of the desk. From a locked drawer at the bottom, he extracted a large folder. He opened it briefly, as if to assure himself one last time of its correct contents, before transferring it to a leather briefcase, which he pulled from another drawer. He then snapped it shut with a loud click; the staccato sound of the clasps locking in place seemed to reverberate across his salon like the sharp ending notes played expressively on a piano keyboard.

He handed the briefcase to Jessica and Alain and said, "Consider the briefcase my gift for the long ride home. I do appreciate you both coming to see me rather than the other way around. I feel most at home around my own possessions these days. I don't like to be away from them for long. I am also happy you got to see my city. If you had more time, I would enjoy showing you some of the sights of Antwerp, but I gather you are both eager to transmit these files to your contacts."

"Yes," Alain said emphatically.

Jessica shot Alain an annoyed look to indicate he need not have worried about her; she had no intention of delaying the transfer of the vital information they now had in their possession for a sightseeing junket about the historic city—even one she had not been to before.

Maes then led them back out to his private lobby by the elevator. "You see these?" he asked, pointing at the paintings that Jessica had first admired upon their arrival at his home. "They are some of what I live for. Averi's museum should offer those who come inside it only the best as well. Don't let Dom Roberts get away with what he has done—even if that's what *he* lives for!"

Back in Paris with Maes's information in tow, Jessica and Alain immediately worked to set up another private conference with

Inspector Lanier. After having some difficulty at first con-
necting with the busy inspector, a meeting had finally been arranged at the French detective's office—and at his convenience.
Now they were once again at the Police Judiciaire, seated in
front of the inspector's generous desk, waiting for him to return
from yet another meeting that he had said could not be delayed,
according to Pecor's report.

"May I get you coffee while you wait for Inspector Lanier?"
Pecor asked politely.

"No thank you. We're fine," Jessica said as Alain also shook
his head.

Jessica saw Pecor give her an encouraging smile, and she
wished the younger inspector were the one in charge whom they
were dealing with instead of the much less approachable Lanier.
But she knew that Alain was quite comfortable with Lanier's
style, and that reassured her to accept the current situation.

Alain now held the briefcase Maes had given them in
Antwerp. The supple leather case sat firmly across his knees.
Its brass metal clasps were shut tightly on either side of its edge,
just waiting to be snapped open on Lanier's entrance to his
office. They had already looked at the extensive papers that
Maes had referred to as his "little proof" of his concerns; they
were inside the case, and they seemed to confirm what Mason's
research had previously provided. True to what they had promised Maes, they hadn't shared the documents with Deschamps
or anyone else, despite their trust of the accountant, but had kept
the papers under wraps for Lanier's sole experienced perusal.

The door to the office then opened, and Jessica quickly
turned her head around to see the burly frame of Inspector
Lanier enter the room. He appeared just as she remembered
him to be—the same, slightly disheveled look and those bushy
black eyebrows that seemed to shade his eyes from any deep

outside inspection. Something was different, though; he was actually smiling at her—she was certain of it. It wasn't a broad smile or a particularly kindly one by any means, but there definitely was one on his lips.

"Bonjour, Dr. Shepard. Inspector Raynaud. It is good to see you both. I hope Pecor has made you comfortable."

Jessica was flabbergasted by the detective's newfound courtesy, and she thought that his other meeting must have been a satisfactory one to have left him in such an obviously contented mood.

"When you contacted me, I checked on the analysis of the documents you gave me previously. I will tell you that our analysis agreed completely with yours. Something has been amiss, of that I am now sure. Now, I understand you have additional documents to show me. May I see them at this time?"

Alain pulled out Maes's papers and handed them across the desk to Lanier's waiting hands. Jessica watched the two detectives briefly assess each other during the exchange; it reminded her of a prisoner exchange at a guarded border crossing. All that was needed to complete the image was two groups of men in fedoras and trench coats on either side of a barrier fence at midnight. She had to shake her head to remove the mental picture from her racing mind.

Lanier continued to scan the papers as he nodded his head up and down. This series of gestures went on for at least several minutes as Jessica couldn't control her foot from tapping impatiently against the floor of the office. She hoped no one else in the room noticed it before she managed to get her foot under control.

"These look consistent with what we have already discovered," he finally said. "You should both know that we were also able to get our hands on a few of the museum's inventory invoices for some pictures that don't seem to exist, interestingly enough." He hesitated a moment, as though to allow his words to sink in totally for effect, and then continued. "Although, of course, what you have brought me will need to be formally analyzed on my end, as the previous ones were."

"Will that take long?" Jessica asked anxiously.

"No. But if they are consistent, it will make it even easier for me to question M. Roberts about them. That is, of course, the obvious next step. What we have so far only suggests embezzlement. It doesn't totally prove it. If we had found double records, that would have made a stronger case. At this time, what I suggest is that you both remain in easy contact with my office. I promise I will make *your case*"—again, he smiled—"a priority."

He then turned to Jessica as if having sensed her initial distrust of him all along, which she had to admit was beginning to fade so that her assessment of him was more in line with Alain's instincts. Lanier then said in a low, deep voice, "I want justice for M. Henri as much as you do, and it will be obtained. You may count on that, young lady."

14

The Waiting Begins

Waiting for Inspector Lanier's call was even more difficult a task than Jessica had thought it would be, so she was extremely grateful that Alain had invited her to join him and Odette to attend a musical evening at the Deschampses' home that night. Jessica hoped it would help pass the time. Marie Deschamps' mother, Suzanne, was having a string quartet entertain her guests at the family's townhouse in Vincennes. It was imparted to Jessica with some amusement that these musical evenings were apparently not an infrequent occurrence; Suzanne reportedly liked to consider herself a noble patron of the arts within her own growing social circle, and in which she was reluctant to make a false step. She had insisted that Odette, her father, and his American friend, who she learned was newly arrived in Paris, be invited to enjoy spending the evening with her family and be part of the select audience expected to attend the concert.

Jessica applied the final touches of makeup to her face. Then she began to critically assess her appearance in the long mirror that was conveniently attached to the back of her bedroom closet door. She had chosen a simple, knee-length black dress and black pumps with kitten heels. At the very last minute, she had added a double string of cultured pearls to encircle her neck; luckily, she had thought to bring the necklace along with her on the trip. The pearls glistened about her throat and brought out the healthy tan on her face and neck, which was steadily deepening due to the time she had been spending outdoors lately.

As she looked up and down at her own reflection in the mirror, she was very satisfied that her costume would be most appropriate for the evening's planned entertainment. All she knew, from what Alain and Odette had already told her, was that Suzanne Deschamps often had this particular group of musicians—two violins, one viola, and one cello player—at her intimate gatherings, and she usually instructed them to play Mozart pieces for her guests.

"Casual but elegant. Don't you think, my dear?" Jessica said to herself before giving her hair one last sweep with her brush and grabbing a light wrap to cover her bare shoulders. She left her apartment, and as the elevator deposited her in the lobby, she saw Madame Clair. The woman was, as frequently was the case, standing guard by the open door to her *loge de concierge*. Jessica had already learned the concierge would do this whenever she heard the elevator rattle down to the lobby, so as not to miss a trick.

"But you are not going out unescorted?" she asked, looking shocked at the very prospect.

"No, Madame Clair. My friends are picking me up just outside."

"Well, that is much better. You had me worried for a moment." She gave Jessica a click of her tongue and then a congratulatory nod of approval before reentering her apartment, seemingly relieved, or possibly actually disappointed, that it would be unlikely that there would be any further disturbance to her quiet night of watching her favorite television shows in her living room.

Once outside and aware that she also wasn't eager to be lurking by herself on a Parisian street dressed as she was, Jessica thankfully soon saw the car carrying Alain and Odette pull up to the curb in front of her.

"You're exactly on time. Much appreciated," Jessica said.

"I would have come up," Odette said, leaning out the passenger window. "Papa thought that was going to be the plan."

"I was eager. That's all. What can I say? Anyway, no matter. I'm here, and so are you."

Odette immediately popped out of the passenger seat of the little car and effortlessly installed herself in the back. It ran through Jessica's mind that the girl's easy relinquishment of her position in the car next to her father was a reassuring sign; if Jessica hadn't received one before, she now knew she was totally accepted by Odette. The teen seemed content and almost totally recovered from the shock she had gotten by witnessing Mason's badly broken body lying on the museum's marble floor so recently.

Jessica got in next to Alain, who gave her the second appreciative glance she had received for the evening. But he didn't say a word and merely started the car. Soon, they were driving through the darkened streets, which were illuminated by tall streetlamps and bright neon signs, once again heading toward Vincennes. The Deschamps lived not far from Odette's home. Alain was still also staying with his daughter nearby because his ex-wife, Josephine, and her new husband, Claude Dabry, hadn't yet returned from vacation, so their address was still Alain's for the moment.

As the car drove along, Odette began to chat spiritedly from the back seat, and her animated chatter drifted over to the front of the car. "Marie's home is a little bigger than ours. Marie's father works such long hours as an accountant that Marie told me her mother has taken to sponsoring struggling artists to keep herself occupied. Marie complains that none of them are good looking enough for her to take an interest in them, but her mother chose this group because Suzanne's old cello instructor recommended them to her. They weren't bad when I last heard them, but Suzanne always has them play the same old pieces from Mozart ... again and again and again. Ugh!"

"Don't you like Mozart, Odette?"

"Oh, I do, but after a while, *how much* Mozart can you listen to? *Really! Be honest!*"

Jessica stole a furtive glance at Alain only to see a slight smile curve his lips, and she was relieved to realize she wasn't alone in her obviously antiquated taste in music. She turned her head over her shoulder and gave Odette a sympathetic nod, valiantly managing to suppress her own impending smile.

When the car pulled up in front of the elegant townhouse where the Deschampses lived, Jessica strained her visual capacity to size it up for herself. It was a two-story, tan stucco home sequestered behind a double wrought iron gate; the gate had been thrown open wide in anticipation of the expected guests' arrival. There was a small cobblestone courtyard in front of the house surrounded by encroaching dark shrubbery on both sides. The door to the townhouse was open and lit from within. An extremely tall, very thin woman with a head of thick auburn hair that managed to be illuminated by the light behind her and that seemed to have more bulk than she did was standing just outside of the open door to greet her guests.

"That's Suzanne," Alain said, taking a deep breath like a diver heading under water for an extended period of time.

He then squeezed the car into the last remaining free corner of the front courtyard that was not yet parked up by the many high-end European cars, and the three got out of Alain's car to greet the hostess in her home.

"*Bonsoir.* Welcome," Suzanne said. She quickly ushered them inside.

The hallway stretched back from the front door to numerous rooms beyond it. There was a golden mirror over a side table into which Suzanne appeared to intermittently shoot glances of herself, particularly after first assessing her American guest's attire for the evening. Suzanne was herself outfitted in a tiny black suit that allowed her long, thin limbs to stretch for miles under the extremely short hem length of her skirt. Jessica detected in Suzanne's confident smile, which she flashed after removing her gaze from the mirror and turning her attention back to Jessica, Alain, and Odette, that the hostess was satisfied.

"Come in and find seats in the salon as quickly as you can. The quartet is still tuning up their instruments, but soon they will start the program. Emmanuel! Emmanuel!" She abruptly turned her head away from her new arrivals, and in an instant, the accountant who had been of such assistance to them materialized from another room as though pulled out like a rabbit from a magician's hat.

"Come in. Come in," Emmanuel said. "Odette, Marie is in her bedroom. I know you would prefer to be with her instead of with us. Go on up. She's waiting for you." He cast a sheepish look at his wife, who appeared to be too distracted by the necessary arrangements of the evening to even notice her husband's appearance on the scene, let alone the fact that at least one of her guests was decamping out of range of the concert.

Emmanuel led Jessica and Alain into a large salon. It was already set up with delicate chairs with gilded bamboo backs; the white leather seats were arranged in a semicircle around the group of four musicians, whose more superficial attributes Marie had, by history, so disparaged. The musicians were busy arranging their music stands and settling into place. As they inspected their bows and made final adjustments to the pegs on their various instruments, Jessica, Alain, and Emmanuel grabbed three seats together.

"Don't worry," Emmanuel whispered. "I don't know anyone in what Suzanne calls *the group* either."

In the audience, there were an assemblage of persons of middle age dressed in a variety of black: black dresses and black suits. Jessica didn't know whether to feel reassured about her choice of outfit or disappointed that she was now part of the herd.

"Suzanne met them through her cello lessons, and now they come to all her recitals. At least they fill up the chairs and leave me be, so I'm content," he added.

Just then Suzanne entered the salon. "Bonsoir. Bonsoir. We will be speaking English tonight for the benefit of one of our guests." The hostess of the evening took one long moment to look pointedly at Jessica, who no longer felt one of *the group*, before she continued speaking. "Tonight, we will be treated to a musical evening devoted entirely to that great master, Mozart."

Jessica imagined she heard Alain stifle a chuckle. Suzanne then made each musician stand up and take a bow in turn as she introduced him to the audience. Soon after, the first lilting strains of classical music began to waft through the room. She then sat next to her husband, with Jessica and Alain on the other side of him, so that Suzanne managed to form a physical barrier between the three and the rest of the guests, as though she was not going to take any chances that any guests of her husband might mingle in her set.

The musicians did their upmost to do service to the genius

of the compositions. Very soon the sound of a pin dropping on the floor would have been heard in light of the total lack of extraneous sounds in the room other than those coming from the quartet's bows upon their strings. The audience was fully concentrated on their playing, and Suzanne seemed content in the success of her evening's entertainment.

"I didn't hear anything further from you both, so I assume what I found in those files did the trick?" Emmanuel asked in a whisper about fifteen minutes into the concert during what appeared to be a short break in the music.

"Sh." Suzanne snapped between her teeth and threw her husband a withering look that would have melted ice.

Several minutes passed, and Emmanuel valiantly tried again, although first he assured himself that his wife was now once more totally transfixed by the music. "My analysis was correct, wasn't it?"

Jessica couldn't resist the temptation and whispered back, "We got additional documents that we think verify what you thought."

"That's great!"

"Sh." This time it came from one of *the group*. He was a thin man wearing a shiny black suit with pant legs short enough to reveal his tanned, sockless feet shod in black patent leather loafers.

Again, after waiting a few minutes, Emmanuel plowed on. "What bothers me is if I saw it and you think your friend saw it, then why didn't Jacques Charles see it also? He is Dom Roberts's uncle, so you have to wonder. But still—"

"Emmanuel! Sh!" Suzanne now practically spat out the words under her breath, and she looked like she was going to imbed one of her narrow, three-inch black heels into her husband's tender shin at any moment.

"Let's get out of here; let's go into the kitchen," her husband said, jerking his head over to the other side of the salon that led to the culinary wing of the townhouse. He gently slid out of his seat and silently evacuated Jessica and Alain from the room. He pointedly ignored the now icy stare of his wife that matched those of the others. The musicians ignored their hasty departure, as though it wasn't the first time they had lost part of their audience in the midst of their performance.

Once in the brightly lit kitchen at the back of the house and sitting around an enormous central island with numerous copper pots that dangled overhead from a metal rack and looked like they had never been put to the fire, Jessica spoke. "Emmanuel, I think you make a good point. The family connection between Dom Roberts and Jacques Charles had slipped my mind, I must admit that. What do you think about it, Alain?"

"I think, as I've said before, let's first see what Lanier comes up with. Roberts is closer to the situation at present than Charles is. Lanier will most likely start there. We can worry about Charles at a later time."

"I don't know," Jessica started. "I wonder if we should—"

"Let it rest for now, Jessica." He placed his hand on her shoulder, and she could feel the gentle pressure through her thin wrap. "This isn't the time or the place for this discussion."

Emmanuel looked disappointed. Jessica wasn't sure if it was because his accounting nose was being taken off the scent or because they now had no other choice but to return to the salon, from which the thunderous applause of Suzanne and her *group* signaled the conclusion of yet another of Suzanne Deschamps's gala concerts.

"Odette, I'm so very, very glad your father let you stay over at my house tonight," Marie said to her best friend as the two teenagers giggled together in French.

Each was tucked up in one of two twin beds with brass headboards. And mountains of down pillows, some of which had been thrown off from the beds, were scattered on the thick pile carpet on the floor. They were still up in Marie's bedroom where they had been passing the time together. The concert had finally finished for the night, and the house was now quiet. All invitees, except for Odette, had departed. Marie had enough experience with her mother's post-concert migraines to know that if she approached Suzanne just as she was preoccupied with escorting her guests out the door, Marie would meet no resistance to one more sleepover with a good friend. The girl's tried-and-true technique of getting what she wanted had paid off beautifully.

Marie was somewhat more sophisticated in her outlook on the world than her friend from school, Odette. And, as close as the two girls were, enjoying extended time together whenever they could, Marie also wanted to get the answers to some questions she had. Marie attributed her own social maturity to having inherited her mother's cosmopolitan taste combined with her father's analytical mind. Odette certainly was an extremely bright girl; she inevitably excelled at their lycée even more than Marie did. But Marie knew her friend was at a disadvantage with her father living most of the time across the Atlantic in Montreal. Also, Josephine and Claude Dabry, Odette's mother and stepfather, were not quite successfully filling the void that had been left for her friend since her father and mother had divorced.

Marie loved to gossip. It was a trait that she got from her mother rather than from her father, who could be *très secret*, at least when it came to the complicated business matters of his clients. Marie knew this sleepover was her very best chance at parsing out what she could about the relationship between Odette's father, Alain, and the American woman he had been so solicitous of that evening. Gossiping was one of the few things Marie had in common with her mother. And as much as her mother's personality annoyed her daughter sometimes, particularly her mother's need for musical recitals that seemed to go on almost every weekend of the year, at other times the teenager enjoyed the chance to confide in her. And if Marie had a juicy tidbit to throw her mother's way occasionally, the mother-daughter bond tightened, and Marie would be sure to reap the benefits when she so chose.

"Odette, so what's the story between your papa and this Jessica woman?"

"What do you mean?"

"Well, come on, your Mama and Papa Claude are away, and your Papa Alain brought her here tonight. Don't tell *me* that they're just good friends. They seemed pretty comfortable with each other."

"Marie, you know Suzanne invited them to come."

"Oh, I know that. But I overheard Suzanne and Emmanuel talking before the concert, and I'm just repeating what I *might* have overheard. Besides, as I said, they seemed pretty chummy, if you ask me about it. That's all I'm saying. And you're here, and he's taking her home. Now, what do *you* think is going to happen? Really, Odette! Sometimes you're too precious for words! But that's why you're my best friend."

"Marie, so are you, but why don't you save your movie scripts for the cinema!"

"Maybe I will. Maybe I will."

15

Lanier Is on the Case

Inspector Lanier received the report that he had been waiting for. It was the detailed analysis of the papers that Raynaud and the American lady doctor had given him to review. The analysis had come back sooner than he had hoped. Lanier had been constantly berating his junior partner, Pecor, to be sure to stay on top of the department's accountant, who was reviewing the papers; all breaks by that diligent but very slow-paced man were to be limited in order to make Lanier's priority the accountant's priority. It had obviously paid off.

Now Lanier held the expected report in his thick fingers. As he slowly turned the pages over one by one, he clicked his tongue roughly against the roof of his mouth in disgust. He didn't like corruption in any form, public or private; it was this particular distaste that had led him to choose his current line of work in the first place. Lanier also didn't like having to occasionally navigate the difficult waters of political expediency; it was a course he usually tried to avoid setting. And, in his long years of service at the Police Judiciaire, he had learned what he could and what he could not accomplish. In this case, he felt he now had enough documentation to stand on solid ground, and that made him feel good.

He put the report down to one side of his cluttered desk and picked up the phone. He dialed the number he had previously obtained. Soon, he heard the click, confirming that the connection had gone through.

"Bonjour," said the voice on the other end of the line.

After confirming he had reached his target, Lanier said in French, "Monsieur Roberts, this is Inspector Lanier with the Police Judiciaire. What time would be convenient for me to speak with you today?"

"What is this in reference to, Inspector? Have you made any headway into your investigation of Mason Henri's suicide?"

"Well, Monsieur Roberts, that aspect of the case is a specific matter that is still under some investigation. But there are other matters, in particular some concerning Musée Averi, for which your input could possibly shine an explanatory light. In that way, I hope to obtain a greater understanding of events that might have led to the unfortunate death of M. Henri."

There was an almost audible pause on the other end of the line and then a terse reply. "Inspector, I am free at two o'clock."

"Excellent. May we expect you to appear at the Police Judiciaire at that time? I will make myself free then to accommodate you."

"Yes, Inspector. You may expect to see me there at that time."

As Lanier replaced the phone into its cradle, the door to his office opened, and Pecor stepped into the room. "Is he going to show up, do you think?" the younger detective asked his more experienced partner.

"We shall see. We shall see. Only time will tell us that."

When two o'clock arrived and then passed, Lanier and Pecor were still waiting for Roberts in Lanier's office. Both men were seated so as to be able to watch the large clock on the side wall that Lanier still insisted on maintaining there. It had been a gift to Lanier from his very first partner when Lanier had only been about Pecor's age and only had his level of experience. That original partner had long since retired, as had a few others, good and bad. But even though the clock was now a bit of an anachronistic timepiece that was often a source of amusement to his coworkers, it had followed Lanier through his various offices at the Police Judiciaire. For the past few years, it had hung in its current spot of prominence on the wall near his desk.

Lanier liked the way the hands of the old faithful clock slowly moved around the luminous dial, and he religiously replaced the batteries in the back of the device whenever the hands stopped moving in a circle. Keeping their slow, relentless, clockwise movement going was a constant reminder to him that methodical progress in the right direction almost always leads to the desired result. If he had learned one thing over the years, it was that patience was usually rewarded, and patience he certainly had. He had always had it.

"So, Jules, it looks as though we must pay a personal visit to M. Roberts. Don't you think?" Lanier did not really expect Pecor to answer him—neither did Pecor, for the matter—but Lanier liked to give his younger partner a little sign of respect, if only now and then.

The two men each got up from their chairs and headed out of the office. They both knew it was time to advance to the next phase of the investigation of the recent events at Musée Averi.

The Musée Averi's security guards, Aleixo and Louis, were unpleasantly surprised to learn that the two detectives from the Police Judiciaire were once again back on the museum's premises. It was a source of some consternation for both of them. At first, Aleixo was very worried that his assistance to the pretty little Odette might have landed him in some heap of trouble that might cost him his job. He had cast suspicious eyes at his colleague, Louis, to try to determine if his coworker had reported any odd behavior on Aleixo's part to the museum, but Aleixo had been reassured by the other man's seemingly innocent demeanor under close perusal. He was even more reassured when it became clear to him that Inspector Lanier was only concerned with the whereabouts of the pompous M. Roberts and not of either of the museum's hardworking security guards.

His conversation with Lanier was being conducted in French, and Aleixo was glad that his command of that language was now almost as good as that of his native Portuguese. He wouldn't have liked to be at any disadvantage whatsoever under the stern gaze of Lanier. The last thing Aleixo wanted was to have to struggle to find the correct word in any interaction with that gruff detective.

"Inspector, all I know is that M. Roberts told the office he was not feeling well and would not come to the museum today. I was standing right by the reception desk when he called. I heard the conversation. He wasn't going to his office at La Défense either.

"Give me his home address then. I'll take that," Lanier said brusquely.

"Yes." Aleixo turned away and grabbed the yellow slip of paper on which the receptionist was hurriedly writing the desired information. It was a small square of paper, and in his agitation, Aleixo almost dropped it, but he managed to catch the fluttering square before it hit the desk and handed it to the detective. Aleixo had no desire to get on the wrong side of Lanier; he didn't look like someone who would take easily to being crossed, even inadvertently.

"Merci" was the only further word he heard before the two detectives left the museum.

He could finally breathe a deep sigh of relief and head back to drink a cup of coffee to brace him up, which by this time he felt he totally deserved.

Lanier and Pecor stood together in front of the entrance to an apartment building in the Champs-Elysées quarter of Paris. It was a building of five levels and considerable width. Lanier checked the address one more time against that written on the paper in his hand and was satisfied they had come to the right spot. He had never before made the stupid mistake of invading a wrong address in his long career, and he had no intention of ever making such a simple mistake.

"Let's hope this is going to be an easy one, Pecor." The inspector was now at that stage of life when he could still run almost as fast as Pecor—if he had to. But he was also acutely aware of the price that would need to be paid to his knees and back the following day for the cost of the required jaunt. He sighed as, with his intuitive eyes, he saw some small sympathy in those of his younger partner. "No, Pecor. As I think about it, I don't feel it will be after all."

The two detectives opened the double doors to the building and went into the vestibule, which was lined with white-and-brown-streaked marble on both the walls and the floors. Even their rubber-soled shoes seemed to echo too loudly as they walked across the entrance hall toward the metal-grilled elevator that was perched to one side of the lobby; it was across from the start of the main staircase on the other side. After the door to the elevator enclosed them inside its grill, Pecor pushed down hard on the button for Dom Roberts's floor. The small elevator climbed up slowly from level to level, seeming to struggle somewhat in its quest to reach its goal. Just before it finally came to a halt, Lanier's trained ears heard a soft noise coming from outside the cage.

"*Écoute!*" he whispered harshly to his partner. In an instant, he knew he was right; they were going to be in for a chase. A part of him still couldn't wrap his mind around the fact that Roberts hadn't realized that if he didn't show up at Lanier's office, they would come to him. But then Lanier had also learned that sometimes the most unexpected thing turns out to be the expected. He often wondered if it was just the human tendency, encouraged by mystery novels and the cinema, to hide in plain sight. He silently cursed. Then he looked at Pecor and jerked his head at the other man in command. But before Pecor could react, Lanier was impatiently grabbing at the door himself to pull it open wide. As the two detectives rushed out of the confining space, they were both able to catch sight of Dom Roberts running across the landing to the curved staircase directly across from them.

"*Arrêt,*" Lanier yelled. But even as the word flew out of his mouth, he knew that the figure fleeing down the stairs would ignore him. It was what he expected.

All that the inspector heard in response to his fiat was the reverberating sound of Roberts's escaping steps down the stairs from level to level, becoming more distant with each passing moment. The two detectives ran down the stairs in hot pursuit of their quarry.

Pecor reached the bottom only slightly before the older Lanier, whose own physical reserves always still seemed to fulfill his body's desired needs in short order whenever called upon in an emergency. The men bounded out of the apartment building and into the street after Roberts.

"Do you see him?" Pecor called out as they fought to identify their target among the many other heads of the people in the busy Paris streets around them.

All they could make out was the wave of bodily collisions in front of them. Roberts was running heedlessly into pedestrians in his way in extreme haste, and they were forced to do the same to keep up with him.

"There he is," Lanier finally yelled.

The two detectives wound through the streets and avenues, down Avenue Franklin Delano Roosevelt to Avenue Champs-Elysées and after that to Avenue Winston Churchill. Suddenly, Lanier had no doubt as to where Roberts was heading. He didn't know why he did, but he did. It flashed through his mind that it was just what he would expect of such a dramatic individual—a fitting final dramatic gesture. Roberts was definitely heading toward Pont Alexandre III.

"Come on," he yelled to his partner.

Even as he continued to chase Roberts, something inside him made Lanier feel a twinge of admiration for his prey, who was choosing the most extravagant bridge in Paris that spanned the Seine for that gesture. Lanier knew it was to be a final statement of defiance of authority in one who obviously believed there was no right for him to be constrained by it.

Lanier spotted the dome of Les Invalides and couldn't help thinking of the tomb of Napoleon that was sheltered there. And involuntarily, the thought made him slow down, so what he saw next came to him almost as though in slow motion, as in a movie. The final cinematic scene was that of Dom Roberts, diving off the large deck arch bridge to plunge far beneath the transverse extension.

But when Lanier reached the bridge, he didn't see Roberts's body hit the water as he had expected he would. Instead, the body flew off the bridge only to land with an agonizing thud that reverberated into the detective's ears on top of a boat carrying cruisers exploring Paris by the Seine. The boat had suddenly emerged from the shelter of the bridge above it, and it now served as an ignominious final resting place for Roberts's motionless body.

16

The Case Appears Closed

Jessica and Raynaud were standing close by Inspector Lanier's side as they peered over the edge of the Pont Alexandre III down to the murky waters below. Roberts's body had been taken away, and the cruise boat upon which his body had so grotesquely landed was now moored at the side of the flowing river. Its horrified passengers had been already discharged from the vessel to give their various witness statements to the police, who had also arrived at the scene.

"Thank you, Inspector, for letting us know so quickly what happened here," Jessica said grimly. She now had such conflicting thoughts running through her mind that her brain was in a tumult. On one hand, she felt vindicated that her suspicions about Dom Roberts had been proven correct; on the other hand, she felt deep remorse that yet one more life was now over, particularly—she also had to admit guiltily to herself—without any opportunity to learn what additional information he would have provided to them. She was also aware that she was slowly coming to grow ever more respect for the brusque French detective, Inspector Lanier, who Alain all along had seemed to have such solid confidence in.

Inspector Lanier failed to acknowledge Jessica's remark of

appreciation except to say in his usual stone-dry manner, "I gather he hoped to make an escape and overestimated his athletic abilities. Or failing that, he wanted, at the very least, to make a truly dramatic exit from this earth."

Jessica looked at Alain, and she detected in his silence that there was something still troubling her companion. His subtle frown reminded her of the expression he had worn at one point during the concert at Emmanuel and Suzanne Deschamps's home. Then he had listened to Emmanuel's attempts at conversation during Suzanne's concert. Jessica remembered what Emmanuel had said: the accountant was troubled by the fact that Jacques Charles's analysis had been so dissimilar to his own assessment. She suddenly wondered if that same thought was now also running through Alain's analytical mind.

It was all so pat, wasn't it? The loose ends had been tied up almost too perfectly with Roberts apparently embezzling funds and having met his end while attempting to avoid the consequences of his actions. There was a gap in the solution they had come to. She felt it. And without a word between herself and Alain, she instinctively knew that he felt it also.

"But, Inspector Lanier, I'm not satisfied by this," Jessica finally said.

"What do you mean? Why would you not be?"

"I think you misunderstand me." She looked at Alain to see if he would stop her from proceeding, but she didn't notice any sign in his face that he thought she shouldn't go on with her own dialogue. "We were told that Roberts has an uncle who used to work at Musée Averi. Alain—Inspector Raynaud—and I had initially approached him about possible irregularities that Mason Henri might have come upon prior to his death. The uncle, Jacques Charles, assured us that there was nothing wrong that he could see. Don't you think it odd that your office confirmed the very opposite situation, as did the accountant who we had look at the numbers, and indeed as the man who provided the additional documentation, Gabriel Maes?"

"We are aware that M. Charles previously was engaged by the museum. We already looked into that connection, as well as that to his nephew, but haven't found anything to be of concern. M. Charles is considered to be a citizen in good standing from everything we have learned about him."

"But we're then assuming that Roberts acted solely alone and that only he might have been involved in Mason Henri's death," Jessica persisted.

"As to that later item, at this point, we still must assume M. Henri took his own life. And if we are wrong about that, then M. Roberts was the most likely culprit, and he has now paid the ultimate price."

"But," Jessica said before she felt Alain's strong hand on her arm. He obviously wanted to refrain her from further argument. It was clear that, at least for now, the case was considered closed.

"I'm just not satisfied," Jessica repeated to Alain in the kitchen of her apartment. Having left the scene at Pont Alexandre III, they had returned to her apartment to talk further.

"You told me that already. You're repeating yourself."

"I know I did, and I know I am, but it's still true. Maybe Jacques Charles *was* involved, and I just don't think Lanier was listening to me. I'm still not totally sure Lanier isn't covering up for him. My assessment of him keeps blowing hot and cold."

"I find that extremely unlikely."

"Why do you think that? Tell me. I wouldn't mind hearing an assessment that's on more of an even keel."

"Well, for one thing, Lanier has been with the Police Judiciaire for a very long time. I made some inquiries on my own. He has an excellent reputation with the department.

"You said 'for one thing,' so what's the other?"

"The other thing is that even if Jacques Charles was shielding his nephew from prosecution, he now has no further access to the museum. He's got his bookshop to take care of."

"And who's to say how he obtained the money for *that* enterprise? Maybe he was involved in some way even before Roberts. Remember, Emmanuel also thought Charles might have gotten Roberts his position, although he couldn't remember for sure. And even if we say there aren't going to be any further financial irregularities at the museum, what about Mason? What about him? Maybe Jacques Charles had something to do with Mason's death."

Alain looked at Jessica and put his hand out to stop her from pacing back and forth across the length of the kitchen's small dimensions, sitting her down firmly in the chair across from him.

"Jessica, do you really think an elder man like Charles would have been more likely than Roberts to be involved in Mason's death if a murder did happen? And we must also admit, Lanier is correct that suicide hasn't been ruled out."

"But it hasn't been proven either. And let me tell you, I've seen many elderly patients in my time, I'll have you know. And it's quite surprising how some of those, who were the very same age as Charles seemed to be, are quite frail, and others are extremely robust. Maybe when we visited Charles, we just expected to see an old man there—from how he had been described to us by the report of a young person like Odette. Maybe we just didn't notice that he was hardier than we thought."

"I think you're letting your vivid imagination run away with you. You were supposed to be helping your friend, Tom, weren't you? Wasn't that how this all started? Why don't you put that good brain of yours to work by figuring out how to summarize what we have learned for him? Then *he* can use his investigative skills and the information you give him to put pressure on Frédéric Averi. Maybe that way we'll assure his businesses are run as they should be run. It's my guess that *if* Averi was unaware of what was going on at his private museum, he may be equally unaware of similar problems going on at his other holdings, despite his obvious financial success. Maybe he has so much going on that a little, here and there—and, mind you, I say *a little* facetiously—goes unnoticed."

"He did seem to be totally absorbed by his château, didn't he?" Jessica reflected, stopping her dissertation momentarily to reflect on Alain's good points.

"Yes. And you saw that the estate is most likely an enormous financial sinkhole, which didn't seem to faze him much. Jessica, this is something too big to handle alone. You know that."

She sighed. "You're right. Okay. I'll talk to Tom. That's what I'll do."

"Good. Now, I've got to get back to Odette and see how she's doing. Shall we call you later, and we can have dinner together?"

"Yes. Yes, of course. That would be wonderful."

"Fine."

Jessica saw Alain out of her apartment and closed the door behind him. Then she sat down in a chair in the living room.

She had agreed with him, but it hadn't left her content by any means. Once he left, doubt flooded over her like a river, or maybe it was just her usual distaste for any sense of a loss of control of a situation.

She bit her lower lip in frustration and reached for her cell phone, which lay on the desk in the corner of the room. She started to dial Tom as she had promised, but then she stopped abruptly before she tapped out the last digit. She didn't care what Alain or Lanier had said. She was not yet ready to turn this *case* over to anyone else. It wasn't the right thing to do. Even though she had only a brief association with Mason, she had liked the young man. She wasn't able to show the same degree of professional detachment as Lanier, or even Alain. She was too involved, and she knew it. There was no going back.

Without any further moment of hesitation, she found the number for Jacques Charles's bookshop in the Latin Quarter and dialed that number instead. She felt only the tiniest bit of trepidation while she waited for the connection to go through on the other end. A residual part of her wanted him not to answer, but most of her did want him to.

"I'll leave it up to chance," she said softly to herself. "If he picks up the phone, I'll take it as a sign that I'm on the right track, and I'll forge ahead. If he doesn't, I won't."

She heard the first ring, then the second, and then, "Bonjour." It was him.

"Bonjour. Monsieur Charles?"

"Oui."

"This is Jessica Shepard."

"Oh. Hello, Dr. Shepard. How are you? What may I do for you today?"

"Thank you for asking. I'm calling because I realized you

must have heard about your nephew, Dom Roberts, and I wanted to talk to you about it. I'm so sorry."

There was a pause on the other end of the line before he answered, "I wasn't aware you were aware that Dom was my nephew." Again, there was hesitation, and then he continued. "But I do appreciate your call. Yes. The detectives from the Police Judiciaire have been in close contact with me. I am just now taking care of some things so that I may close my shop for the time it takes to make the necessary arrangements. It is a very sad affair. Obviously, this has all been a great shock to me, as I'm sure you can imagine."

"I can certainly understand that. I hate to bother you at a time like this, but I did wish to speak with you. Are you going to be in your shop for a short time longer so that I may see you there?"

"No. I don't think I will be. Perhaps, after all, it would be a better idea for me to come to you. I need to be doing things and moving about. In any case, I can't stay still. Tell me where you are, and I will meet you there. It will be better that way."

Jessica debated his offer with herself only for a moment because she knew that the only way not to appear suspicious was to be agreeable. "I'll give you my address."

After she hung up the phone, she went back to her front door and opened it wide. "Better safe than sorry," she muttered. She would keep the door open for her visitor and not close it during the time that he was in her apartment—just in case.

As Jacques Charles hung up the phone, he saw the door to his shop open. A man wearing a shirt with the label of a local courier service that occasionally delivered packages to him entered. The courier gruffly handed him a letter and then left.

Jacques opened the envelope and saw that it contained a letter addressed to him from his nephew, Dom. He must have sent it just before his death. He took his reading glasses out from the inner pocket of his suit jacket and read the letter aloud to himself in French.

Uncle Jacques,

By the time you receive this letter, I will have left, either to parts unknown if I am successful or to a better place if not.

Since my parents died, you have been the one closest to me, always guiding me. I have tried to follow in your footsteps professionally. We always used to joke that you taught me everything I know.

Well, I have failed. I tried to be a faithful follower to M. Averi and to you, but I haven't been as successful in my tasks as you were. And now I know that the noose is tightening around my neck, and I have no reserves to face the consequences.

For the memory of my mother, your sister, and for your willingness to raise me, I forgive you for any mistakes you made to me, as I hope you forgive any mistakes that I made to you.

Your nephew,
Dom

The old man replaced his reading glasses in the inner pocket of his suit jacket. He folded the letter in threes so that two sharp edges formed in the paper. Then he folded it in half again. He placed it in the same jacket pocket so that it was close to his breast before he left the store to meet Dr. Jessica Shepard at her apartment on Boulevard de Courcelles.

Jacques Charles knocked on the open door of Jessica's apartment. The harsh tapping sound jolted her from her inner thoughts. She went over to the newcomer to invite him into her living room. As she approached the older man who was standing by the entrance, she tried to nonchalantly size him up, this time without prejudice from anyone else's prior assessment of him.

Perhaps, she had been letting her vivid imagination run riot. The old man hovering in the doorway didn't look like one bearing her any ill will or one who would be a danger to her by any means. He looked positively crestfallen, which was not unexpected, she thought, considering he had just lost a nephew. Jessica wondered if he had been involved whether he was feeling remorse for financial misdeeds, and if he hadn't been involved if he felt bad for missing them when asked for his evaluation of the relevant numbers. Looking at him now, she certainly couldn't imagine him having had anything to do with Mason's unfortunate demise.

"May I enter?" he asked politely, curving his neck slightly to see beyond the open door and her body in front of it and farther into the apartment.

"Of course, forgive me. Please come in. I don't know what I was thinking. I'm glad you were able to come here. I hope I haven't inconvenienced you. You must have so many things to take care of. How are you holding up?"

"Thank you for the concern. Fairly well. You cannot even begin to know how much there is to do when one is thrown into a situation like this."

"Well, come and sit down inside, and we can talk," she said, motioning for him to come inside.

"That is very kind." M. Charles followed Jessica into the living room. He settled into a comfortable chair and looked around him. Then he said, "You mentioned that you wished to speak to me. May I now ask what it is about?"

Jessica pulled over a chair and sat down directly across from him so as to get the best view of his face while they spoke. "Yes. This is rather a delicate matter. I'm not sure how to begin, but I felt I needed to broach the subject."

"Please feel free to say whatever it is you wish," he said. "I am listening."

"Thank you." Now feeling more unsure of herself than ever but still unwilling to totally discount her concerns, Jessica proceeded cautiously. "You must recall that my friend Alain Raynaud and I initially came to see you requesting information about what Mason Henri might have found before his unfortunate death."

"Certainly I do, but as I previously explained, I found nothing of concern at that time, so I didn't keep the papers I had received from him. If other information has been found to the contrary, which I gather is the case from what I have been told by the Police Judiciaire and what you have just said, let me assure you it was merely an oversight on my part. You must excuse the fading acumen of an older man. It happens to all of us, you know. It will to you one day as well, my dear. Time does not stop for anyone."

As he looked at her, Jessica thought, *Did I just detect his eyes narrow slightly?* Or was she just imagining the first hint of spite in his comment? She decided to ignore the look of his eyes or his comment and just continue on the same tack she had set for herself. "I do not wish to disturb you, but the Police Judiciaire quickly spotted irregularities in the data, which were confirmed with additional documents."

"Additional documents, did you say?"

"Yes, I did. Is it possible that you may have wished to shield your nephew in some way? Might have Mason been wondering the same? Is that why he went to you, even though you were long gone from your job working at the museum?"

She knew that mentioning Mason's name would now put him on guard, but something inside her still wanted to give the older man a way out of the situation. She wanted to hear his explanation with her own ears, but as she stopped speaking, the face across from her, whose eyes she had so recently thought might be narrowing, seemed to suddenly take on the appearance of a dog ready to bite. And his hands, though showing ravages of age with papery skin flexed over them, were tightly clenched to the ends of either side of his armchair. He was intermittently opening and closing his hands as if to release the pressure building up inside his body.

All at once, Jessica wondered if her initial qualms about meeting him alone in her apartment had been right. She had been foolish to proceed as she had on her own. But, after a moment, he seemed to relax and, with relief, so did she.

"May I ask for a cup of tea?" he asked quietly. "It seems this talk has unnerved me after all. I will be happy to answer any questions you have after some sustenance. I didn't take the time to have anything to drink before I came here to speak with you." He laughed softly as though embarrassed by the request.

Jessica felt even more relieved at his polite request and said, "Of course. Forgive me again. Why don't you come into the kitchen? We'll have some tea together."

She then led him into the kitchen at the back of the apartment, but on the way, she still didn't close the front door but left it wide open. Better to be safe than sorry she had thought, and she still felt that way. She filled the teakettle with water from the tap and placed it on the stove, while M. Charles sat down on the chair by the kitchen window. He peered out through the glass panes at the garden below.

"We're lucky the weather is still quite pleasant. Aren't we?" he said. "The city of Paris can be brutally hot at times this late in the year."

"Yes. I've been told about that. One thing to be grateful for, I guess."

Charles stood up shakily to get a better look at the concierge's cherished garden in the back of the building. Madame Clair had recently been working the gardener very hard. Jessica had gleaned that from the stream of verbal commands she had recognized as coming from the elderly woman, which Jessica had intermittently heard coming up from below. She watched Charles pull glasses out of the inner pocket of his jacket. As he did so, a piece of paper nearly fluttered out of his pocket, but he put it back into his jacket. He moved closer to the window to get a better look at the view, leaning against the frame for support.

"Be careful," she said as she fiddled with lighting the stove. She was still unfamiliar with its workings and thought back longingly to her stove in her house in Connecticut, which seemed to be so much easier to get going. "The frame is a little weak. I'm waiting to have it repaired," she added absentmindedly.

Even before the words were out of her mouth, she realized she had said exactly the wrong thing. She turned away from the stove to see that, in an instant, Charles had pushed his entire body against the window. It came loose easily from the wall, only to crash down just moments later and land on the ground below with a sickening thud and the sound of shattering glass.

He then swung his body around back toward her and somehow seemed to have regained all the lost strength of his youth. His arms suddenly encircled Jessica, and she immediately knew she was in a violent life-and-death struggle that she couldn't lose. She felt herself giving up ground to the man and wished she'd had a chance to grab the heavy teakettle before he had set upon her. It would have been useful as a defensive weapon. But he had taken her by total surprise as she had fiddled with the tea, and she felt herself being relentlessly dragged toward the open gap in the wall where the window had served as a safety barrier just moments before.

She fiercely fought him, as well as her confusion, and struggled to get her mind to concentrate on her own best defense. She had only the strength of her hands as she was thrown off balance. She used her hands as best she could to claw frantically at the edges of the window frame and try to find anything firm to grab onto for support.

Then, as if in slow motion, she heard him lash out in anger through clenched lips. "I loved Dom. He was the only family I had left in this world. I wasn't going to allow an upstart like Mason hurt him. How lucky that I kept my key to the museum. It gave me an easy way to show him who was still in charge. But believe me, I felt worse about what I did to him than anything I might do to you. You should have learned by now to mind your own business."

But Jessica could only hear the words through a fog, and all she could focus on was the sight of the patches of gray pavement down in the garden below; there was a dizzying kaleidoscope of greens, browns, and grays beneath her. It was a crazy moment, and unfathomably, all at once, her mind flashed back to the helicopter ride she had taken with Alain on their journey to the Château Averi. The swirling motion of the helicopter blades she remembered from that ride seeming to match the rotary motion of her brain under the physical assault against her body; the colors somehow were also similar as they circled before her, and she feared falling toward them. Then she realized something was very different. Down below, she could clearly see the figure of Madame Clair, who was looking up at her as Jessica struggled against Charles's newfound strength; even from the height of her apartment, Jessica could see that there was pure horror on the kindly woman's face that stared up at her.

"*Là-haut. Là-haut.*" Jessica could hear the concierge shouting. "Up there. Up there." But she wasn't yelling to Jessica. She was yelling to men rapidly running across the garden. But how would they get to her Jessica wondered before she heard disconnected voices coming from the front of her apartment.

As she continued to struggle with Charles, she somehow managed to twist her body toward the front of the kitchen, and she could see Lanier, Pecor, and Alain suddenly come upon them. As she worked valiantly to extract herself from the ensuing scrum, she felt more than saw Charles suddenly seem to lose his balance. It was only later that she would wonder if he had let her go on purpose, realizing he would lose the battle, before he fell out the window and hurtled down to the solid ground below.

17

The Picture Is Painted

"How did you ever manage to get here in time?" Jessica asked breathlessly. "I can't believe it!"

She was still in a state of shock. She was sitting next to Alain at the table where, just minutes before, her attacker had been calmly asking for tea before he set upon her. Inspector Lanier was standing in front of her, his large frame backlit by the dim hall light coming from outside the tiny kitchen. As Jessica turned her head away from the two inspectors and back toward the large aperture in her kitchen wall that had previously housed her window, she could see Pecor crouched down low over the body of Jacques Charles. The old man's corpse was lying so still on the ground, hideously distorted from the fall.

Even through the fog of her recent trauma, she could still discern the hysterical tone of Madame Clair's voice as the woman spoke loudly in extreme agitation in the back garden, alternatingly directing her distraught commentary to the young inspector and then to the other police agents who were there. The concierge's anguished words floated up in the still air from the otherwise quiet back garden, and Jessica knew that the woman's connection to her beloved, verdant spot would never be the same again. There was no way now it could be.

"We had a tail on Monsieur Charles, and we were also keeping an eye on you," Lanier explained bluntly. "Your friend Raynaud," he added, jerking his large head in Alain's general direction, "had no confidence in your ability to refrain from contacting M. Charles by yourself. I see he was correct in his assessment."

Did she detect a smile on those thin lips of Inspector Lanier? She was never quite sure with him.

"So we both thought it was just a matter of time until you would reach out to him. We thought we should be prepared for it. I must admit that I did not think you would act so quickly to do so. But Raynaud obviously knows you better than I. He advised me of your resourcefulness and that he thought you would do it, *dans ce moment*."

"Well, I appreciate that, Inspector. I really do. I'll always be grateful."

"Yes, it is lucky for you that I listened to him and quickly set up the tails. I had told you M. Charles was considered a citizen in good standing from everything we had learned about him ... at the time. But additional information came to my attention soon after we spoke. You see this letter?"

Lanier showed Jessica a handwritten note that had been folded in threes and again in half. He straightened out the letter so that Jessica could see it better, although it was written in French.

"My men pulled it out of M. Charles's jacket pocket. Unfortunately, he will have no need of it any longer." The inspector looked briefly at the open window aperture to the garden below as though to emphasize his point. "It's a letter from Dom Roberts to Jacques Charles. It's obviously written in French, and I won't translate the whole letter for you except for this phrase."

He pointed to a line in the letter and read aloud to her in English, "'We always used to joke that you taught me everything I know.' That phrase bothered me. I see you are puzzled. Let me explain. We had obtained a copy of this letter before it was delivered to M. Charles with the help of a courier service that we knew M. Roberts always used to send his correspondence. For this bit of luck, we did have the assistance of M. Averi himself, as they were his company's courier service. You see, there is some back history that you are not aware of.

"M. Averi had, at one time, been *familiar* with Dom Roberts's mother, Jeanne, who was a widow and also Jacques Charles's sister. And no, Dom Roberts was not M. Averi's son. The affair started after M. Roberts was born and ended with Jeanne's death in a car accident. We looked into this further. Apparently, there were some statements made by M. Charles at the time of Jeanne's death that he blamed Frédéric Averi. It seems Jeanne was on her way to rendezvous with M. Averi when the accident occurred. It appeared some of the financial irregularities at Musée Averi, which we only found on further inspection, started at that time. Perhaps M. Charles, who was now responsible for Dom Roberts education and upkeep, felt it was his due."

Lanier took a brief pause in speaking, as though to gather his future words together, although Jessica wasn't sure if it was more likely to give her time to let what he had already told her sink in before he continued.

"M. Charles arranged for Dom Roberts to eventually take over his job at Musée Averi. I do believe from what I've learned that Dom Roberts looked up to M. Averi as a substitute father, and perhaps M. Averi considered Dom Roberts as a type of son. I do not know. But it seems that much of what was taken from the museum without M. Averi's knowledge did go to Château

Averi, although Dom Roberts did obviously keep some for himself. And we have also been looking into some concerns regarding other corporate diversions to the château."

Again, the inspector took a brief pause before going on with his dissertation. "Much of what we had concerning M. Charles was circumstantial speculation. But when he received the letter from the courier and came to see you so soon after, we were concerned events might spin out of control if M. Charles felt in some way you were responsible for his nephew's death. With the history I have so far related to you, it makes sense that they were very close. Of course, we still had no proof regarding the events surrounding Mason Henri's tragic death until you received M. Charles's confession prior to his attack. Now that he is also dead, that aspect of the case is finally closed."

"What a story!" Jessica said after Lanier finally appeared as though he was finished. "Well, I'm glad you came here in time for my sake. That's all I can say."

"You are welcome. But I would suggest next time—if there is one, young lady—that you hold off on taking such matters into your own hands. We really do know what we are talking about, despite whatever else you might think. Justice takes time to get it right, and patience is usually rewarded."

Jessica did not fail to note the not too subtle rebuke she was receiving from the inspector. But she was so grateful to him, and still so shaken up by what had just transpired, that she managed to take no offense.

"I was right about Jacques Charles, though," she said just a moment later, thinking back on events and, as always, unable to totally cede a point in any competition. "You have to both admit that. He wanted to protect his nephew and his family name, so he did the unthinkable in killing Mason. It is just so sadly ironic when you think about it that three men have all fallen to their deaths: first Mason Henri, then Dom Roberts, and now Jacques Charles."

Jessica shook her head as though the recent confluence of violent events was still too much for her to take in and get a handle on so as to control her own tumultuous emotions. Finally she asked, "What is going to happen now?"

Raynaud spoke first. "Tom Martine contacted me awhile back because he needed some assistance with various authorities to get additional information on Frédéric Averi. Averi has some holdings in Canada, where it was easiest for me to help Tom get at what he needed. I also contacted Inspector Lanier, who was simultaneously dealing with Averi's French holdings. Long story short, Averi has now distanced himself, as have most of his investors, from any arms of his companies that had *irregularities*. These power brokers are now either not involved in the development of the questionable holdings or in the operations of them. Going forward, of course, they'll have to assure more oversight because the excuse of having distinct organizations with separate teams of employees won't hold true any longer for any of them. It just won't hold water anymore. But it's early in the process yet; this will all take some time to sort out and resolve."

"I'm glad you two and Tom worked together," Jessica said, realizing that perhaps Alain had been right, and the best results were not necessarily those obtained on one's own. Coordinated teamwork had paid off and saved her life.

"I'm sure your friend Tom Martine's reporting will be crucial in making sure no further gross irregularities occur among Averi Industries," Inspector Lanier said. "M. Martine does have a personal reason to follow through on this front, doesn't he, from what Inspector Raynaud has told me?"

"Yes, he does," Jessica said. "I must admit I didn't realize you could all work together so quickly and efficiently. It's very comforting. But—wait a minute—what about the museum? What's going to happen there?"

"Apparently, Monsieur Averi plans to sell the museum," Lanier said. "It appears his château is his mistress and his museum only his wife."

Jessica looked up at him, and this time definitely could detect a slight trace of amusement on his face before he continued more soberly.

"But he has decided he can only have one true love to lavish his money on. Perhaps, with only one passion in his life, he will not be spread so thin financially, and his other holdings will be allowed to flourish, rather than only be there to primarily generate profits. We can only hope for the best."

"Yes. Let's hope," Jessica said.

"Now, I think we need to get that window fixed," Lanier said as he came over and peered out through the large open gap behind her. "I am now going to join my partner, Pecor, outside. I will send the concierge up to take a look at your window frame. But I think it is now Pecor who needs some rescuing."

This time Jessica was sure. There was a broad smile spreading across the inspector's face.

18

The Final Strokes Are Applied

Jessica, Alain, and Odette sat together in the rear courtyard garden of Musée Averi because Odette had finally returned to her summer internship at the museum. The teenager wanted them to enjoy the pretty spot, now that a semblance of normalcy had returned to their lives. The weather was warm and pleasant and the site so tranquil that it was hard to fathom such distressing events had recently occurred so close by. The museum was now open, and visitors were coming in and out the doors of the building, but so far that day, the courtyard garden was being overlooked by those more interested in the museum's inner contents. So, Jessica, Alain, and Odette were undisturbed where they sat, and their conversation would be private.

Odette had been made aware, in as gentle a way as her father could relate to her, that Mason Henri's killer, Jacques Charles, had been apprehended and had died, as had Dom Roberts, whose financial manipulations had so troubled Mason in the first place. Much of Jessica's near brush with death had been glossed over in Alain's retelling of events to his daughter. The trio were now huddled around a small wooden folding table on which three cups of coffee were cooling in the fragrant air about the garden. And the pungent aroma of coffee was mingling with that of the diverse flowers around them.

"I still haven't totally forgiven your father for not letting me know he was coordinating activities with my friend Tom Martine and with Inspector Lanier without my knowing anything about it," Jessica said half-jokingly to Odette. "Although I guess I shouldn't look a gift horse in the mouth. Your actions did help to tie up the loose ends of this case, Alain."

"Oh, Papa has many layers to him," Odette said. "He's not a gift horse at all. He's quite the onion when you think about it."

"I can see I am being dissected by the doctor and the budding detective," Alain said with mock outrage.

"I'm still not sure what I want to study once I leave the lycée, Papa. I've told you that many times. Art or criminal justice, now which should it be? Let's see." She picked up her coffee, took a small sip, and rolled her eyes up to the sky with a comic gesture that any French mime artist would have applauded and tried to imitate.

"Well, I heard from Tom *myself*, and I won't be so selfish with *my* news, Alain," Jessica said. She waited a minute for dramatic effect and then continued. "Tom's sister, Lucy, is apparently now seeing someone romantically. So I think we can conclude that she's on the mend. Tom says that she seems much less depressed nowadays, and he's confident she'll totally return to her old self, given some more time. Also, Tom has written an article on corporate ethics and philanthropy based on his—and our—experience here, and it has been published. It's been so well received that he's thinking about writing a whole book on the subject. He thinks it will be a shoo-in for publication. So, you see, all our hard work did pay off in the end. It was worth it—even if it did turn out to be more of a harrowing adventure than I thought it would be when I first signed on."

"Oh, really? You were surprised the adventure would be harrowing?" Alain asked.

"Yes," Jessica said before ignoring him further and turning to his daughter. "And, Odette, I just want to add that I think you were so wonderful in helping me and your father. We couldn't have done any of this without you. That goes without saying. I can't thank you enough. Whatever you decide to do with your life, I know you'll be successful at it."

"Well, there's one thing that bothers me. I feel that you and Papa didn't get enough time to see much of my city in a fun way. Now that Mama and Papa Claude are coming back from vacation, I hope you'll both have time on your own. Then, of course, I'll also be able to concentrate on my internship without having to be a detective at the same time, Papa."

"I think you'll have to fully concentrate on your internship because there's going to be some big changes at Musée Averi coming down the pipe," Alain said, not to be outdone.

"What changes?" Jessica asked. "Come on. Say what you have to say. Don't be so mysterious! You're still in the doghouse for not letting me in about you and Tom and Lanier."

"My, you are really pushing the imagery today. Aren't you? Fine, I won't be mysterious. Who do you think may be purchasing Musée Averi? I heard it directly from Lanier who found out all about it from his sources."

"Who?"

"It's Gabriel Maes, our very own helpful diamond dealer from Antwerp, who was so agreeable at providing the additional documents we used to get Lanier totally engaged. It appears that Maes has the necessary funds for the museum's purchase. I think he also plans to merge some of his collection—at least the French pieces—with those of Musée Averi. But I imagine he might be planning to change the name of the museum. I'm sure not for any love of self-promotion!"

"Well, it's funny, but I'm not totally surprised by that," Jessica said. "I guess it all makes sense when you think about it."

Before Jessica could mull over anything more to say about the matter, she saw Aleixo Santos approaching them from inside the museum. He came over to the table the three were sharing in the courtyard. He was still wearing his security guard's uniform, but now Jessica noticed the uniform was impeccably arranged on Aleixo's sturdy frame. Every button was buttoned, and there wasn't a wrinkle to be seen on the material in a single spot. Jessica guessed the news of a potential sale of the museum was not isolated to Lanier and Alain but was also slowly making its way through the gossip circles of the ranks of the employees of the museum. She had a feeling that a stricter form of governance would now be the rule at the museum, especially if Gabriel Maes would be the man now in total charge of it.

"Odette, would you like to join the meeting that's going to start inside? I was asked if you wanted to be included in it," Aleixo said in French.

"Yes, thank you. I would. I'm coming." The teenager got up and said with a broad smile on her lips, "Goodbye, Jessica. It was a spine-tingling adventure of a summer, but I wouldn't have wanted to experience it with anyone else but you and Papa." She leaned over and planted a kiss on either side of Jessica's cheeks, hugged her father tenderly, and then went off with Aleixo to head back inside the museum.

Jessica struggled against a couple of wet tears that were forming in the corners of her eyes and starting to blur her vision as she watched Odette walk away from them.

"So how about it?" Alain asked.

"What?"

"Why don't we take my daughter's advice and spend some more time together and experience Paris as we should have been able to?"

Jessica didn't say another word; neither did Alain. But when he reached across the tiny table between them to take her hand and leaned across it to kiss her, she knew no words were needed.